IMPOSTOR

An Alexander Gregory Thriller

LJ ROSS

ISBN: 978-1-917863-01-8

This edition published in 2025 by Dark Skies Publishing

Author photo by Gareth Iwan Jones

Cover layout and typesetting by
Riverside Publishing Solutions Ltd

Cover artwork by Andrew Davidson

Printed and bound by CPI Goup (UK) Limited

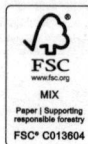

FSC
www.fsc.org
MIX
Paper | Supporting
responsible forestry
FSC® C013604

BOOKS BY LJ ROSS

THE ALEXANDER GREGORY THRILLERS:

THE DCI RYAN MYSTERIES:

THE SUMMER SUSPENSE MYSTERIES:

"There is nothing more deceptive than an obvious fact."

—Sir Arthur Conan Doyle, *The Boscombe Valley Mystery*

PROLOGUE

August 1987

She was muttering again.

The boy heard it from beneath the covers of his bed; an endless, droning sound, like flies swarming a body. The whispering white noise of madness.

Poor, poor baby, she was saying. *My poor, poor baby.*

Over and over she repeated the words, as her feet paced the hallway outside his room. The floorboards creaked as she moved back and forth, until her footsteps came to an abrupt halt.

He hunkered further down, wrapping his arms around his legs, as if the pattern of Jedi knights on his *Star Wars* duvet cover could protect him.

It couldn't.

The door swung open and his mother was silhouetted in its frame, fully dressed despite it being the middle of the night. She strode across the room and shook his coiled body with an unsteady hand.

"Wake up! We need to go to the hospital."

1

The boy tried not to sigh. She didn't like it when he sighed, when he looked at her the 'wrong' way, or when he argued. Even if he did, she wouldn't listen.

She wouldn't even *hear*.

"I'm awake," he mumbled, although his body was crying out for sleep.

He was always sleepy.

"Come on, get dressed," she continued, and he tried not to look directly at her as she scurried about the room, pulling out clothes at random for him to wear. He didn't want to see her eyes, or what was hidden behind them. They'd be dark again, like they were before, and they'd look straight through him.

There came a soft moan from the bedroom next door, and his mother hurried out, leaving him to pull on jeans and a faded *Power Rangers* t-shirt. The clock on the bedside table told him it was three-seventeen a.m., in cheerful neon-green light. If he had the energy to spare, he might have wondered whether the children he'd seen playing in the garden next door ever got sick, like he did, or whether they got to go to school.

He remembered going to school, once.

He remembered liking it.

But his mother said he was too ill to go to school now, and he'd learn so much more at home, where she could take care of him and Christopher.

It wasn't her fault that, despite all her care, neither boy seemed to get any better.

Once, when she thought he was asleep, she'd come in to sit on the edge of his bed. She'd stroked a hand over his hair and told him that she loved him. For a moment, he thought Mummy had come back; but then, she'd moved her mouth close to his ear and told him it was all because Daddy had left them to be with something called a Filthy Whore, and everything would have been alright if he'd never gone away. He hadn't known what she meant. At first, he'd wondered if some kind of galactic monster had lured his father away. Maybe, at this very moment, he was trapped in a cast of bronze, just like Han Solo.

She called his name, and the boy dragged his skinny body off the bed. There was no time to make up fairy tales about his father, or to wonder how other children lived.

Or how they died.

There was more muttering at the hospital.

He could hear it, beyond the turquoise curtain surrounding his hospital bed. Whenever somebody passed by, the material rippled on the wind and he caught sight of the serious-looking doctors and nurses gathered a short distance away.

"*I can't see any medical reason—*" he heard one of them say, before the curtain flapped shut again. "*This needs to be reported.*"

"*There have been cases,*" another argued.

"*One dead already, the youngest in critical condition—*"

The boy tensed as he recognised the quick *slap-slap-slap* of his mother's tread against the linoleum floor.

"Where's my son? Where've you taken him?" she demanded, in a shrill voice. "Is he in there?"

He saw her fingers grasp the edge of the curtain, and unconsciously shrank back against the pillows, but she did not pull it back.

There ensued a short argument, conducted in professional undertones.

"If you really think—alright. Yes, yes, he can stay overnight, so long as I stay with him at all times. But what about Christopher?"

The voices receded back down the corridor as they moved towards the High Dependency Unit, where his younger brother lay against scratchy hospital bedsheets, fighting for his life.

When the boy awoke the next morning, he was not alone.

Three people surrounded his bed. One, he recognised as the doctor who'd snuck him a lollipop the previous night, and she gave him a small smile. Another was a stern-faced man wearing a dark suit that reminded him of his father, and the other was a young woman in a rumpled police uniform with sad brown eyes.

"Hi, there," the doctor said. "How're you doing, champ?"

There was a false note of cheer to her voice that made him nervous.

"W-where's my mum?"

The three adults exchanged an uncomfortable glance.

"You'll see your mother soon," the man told him. "I'm afraid she's had some bad news. You both have."

In careful, neutral tones, they spoke of how his younger brother had died during the night and, with every passing word, the boy's pale, ghostly-white face became more shuttered.

It had happened before, you see.

Last year, his baby sister had died too, before she'd reached her first birthday.

He remembered all the cards and flowers arriving at the house they used to live in; the endless stream of neighbours pouring into his mother's living room to condole and glean a little gossip about their misfortune. He remembered his mother's arm wrapped around his shoulder, cloying and immoveable, like a band of steel.

"*These two are all I have left, now,*" she'd said, tearfully, drawing Christopher tightly against her other side. "*I can only pray that God doesn't take them, too.*"

And, while the mourners tutted and wept and put 'a little something' in envelopes to help out, he'd watched his mother's eyes and wondered why she was so happy.

CHAPTER 1

Ballyfinny
County Mayo, Ireland
Thirty years later

"Daddy, what's an '*eejit*'?"

Liam Kelly exited the roundabout—where he'd recently been cut-up by the aforementioned *eejit* driving a white Range Rover—and rolled his eyes. His three-year-old daughter was growing bigger every day, and apparently her ears were, too.

"That's just a word to describe somebody who…ah, does silly things."

She thought about it.

"Are you an *eejit*, Daddy?"

Liam roared with laughter and smiled in the rear-view mirror.

"It's been said," he admitted, with a wink. "Nearly home now, sugarplum. Shall we tell Mammy all about how well you did in your swimming class, today?"

His daughter grinned and nodded.

"I swam like a fish, didn't I?"

"Aye, you did. Here we are."

It took a minute for him to unbuckle her child seat and to collect their bags, but then Liam and his daughter were skipping hand in hand up the short driveway leading to the front door of their bungalow on the outskirts of the town. It was perched on higher ground overlooking the lough and, though it had been a stretch to buy the place, he was reminded of why they had each time he looked out across the sparkling water.

The front door was open, and they entered the hallway with a clatter of footsteps.

"We're back!" he called out.

But there was not a whisper of sound on the air, and he wondered if his wife was taking a nap. The first trimester was always tiring.

"Maybe Mammy's having a lie-down," he said, and tapped a finger to his lips. "Let's be quiet like mice, alright?"

"Okay," she replied, in a stage whisper.

"You go along and play in your bedroom and I'll bring you a glass of milk in a minute," he said, and smiled as she tiptoed down the corridor with exaggerated care.

When the little girl pushed open the door to her peaches-and-cream bedroom, she didn't notice her mother at first, since she was lying so serenely amongst the stuffed toys on the bed. When she did, she giggled, thinking of the story of Goldilocks.

"You're in my bed!" she whispered.

She crept towards her mother, expecting her eyes to open at any moment.

But they didn't.

The little girl began to feel drowsy after her exertions at the swimming pool, and decided to curl up beside her. She clambered onto the bed and, when her hands brushed her mother's cold skin, she tugged her rainbow blanket over them both.

"That's better," she mumbled, as her eyelids drooped.

When Liam found them lying there a short while later, the glass fell from his nerveless hand and shattered to the floor at his feet. There was a ringing in his ears, the pounding of blood as his body fought to stay upright. He wanted to scream, to shout—to reject the truth of what lay clearly before him.

But there was his daughter to think of.

"C-come here, baby," he managed, even as tears began to fall. "Let's—let's leave Mammy to sleep."

CHAPTER 2

South London
One month later

Doctor Alexander Gregory seated himself in one of the easy chairs arranged around a low coffee table in his office, then nodded towards the security liaison nurse who hovered in the doorway.

"I'll take it from here, Pete."

The man glanced briefly at the other occupant in the room, then stepped outside to station himself within range, should his help be required.

After the door clicked shut, Gregory turned his attention to the woman seated opposite. Cathy Jones was in her early sixties but looked much younger; as though life's cares had taken very little toll. Her hair was dyed and cut into a snazzy style by a mobile hairdresser who visited the hospital every few weeks. She wore jeans and a cream wool jumper, but no jewellery—as per the rules. Her fingernails were painted a daring shade of purple and she had taken time with her make-up, which was flawless. For all the world, she could have been one of the smart, middle-aged women he saw sipping rosé at a wine bar in the city, dipping focaccia bread into small bowls of olive oil and balsamic while they chatted with their friends about the latest episode of *Strictly Come Dancing*.

That is, if she hadn't spent much of the past thirty years detained under the Mental Health Act.

"It's nice to see you again, Cathy. How was your week?"

They went through a similar dance every Thursday afternoon, where he asked a series of gentle, social questions to put her at ease, before attempting to delve into the deeper ones in accordance with her care plan. Though he was generally optimistic by nature, Gregory did not hold out any great hope that, after so long in the system, the most recent strategy of individual and group sessions, art and music therapy, would bring this woman any closer to re-entering normal society—but he had to try.

Cathy leaned forward suddenly, her eyes imploring him to listen.

"I wanted to speak to you, Doctor," she said, urgently. "It's about the next review meeting."

"Your care plan was reviewed recently," he said, in an even tone. "Don't you remember?"

There was a flicker of frustration, quickly masked.

"The clinical team made a mistake," she said.

"Oh? What might that be?"

Gregory crossed one leg lightly over the other and reached for his notepad, ready to jot down the latest theory she had cobbled together to explain the reason for her being there in the first place. In thirty years as a patient in four different secure hospitals, under the care of numerous healthcare professionals, Cathy had never accepted the diagnosis of her condition.

Consequently, she hadn't shown a scrap of remorse for her crimes, either.

"Well, I was reading only the other day about that poor, *poor* mother whose baby died. You know the one?"

Gregory did. The tragic case of Sudden Infant Death Syndrome had been widely reported in the press, but he had no intention of sating this woman's lust for tales of sensational child-deaths.

"Anyway, all those years ago, when they put me in *here*, the doctors didn't know so much about cot death. Not as much as they do now. If they had, things might have been different—"

Gregory looked up from his notepad, unwilling to entertain the fantasies that fed her illness.

"Do you remember the reason the pathologist gave for the deaths of your daughter, Emily, and your son, Christopher? Neither of them died following Sudden Infant Death Syndrome, as I think you're well aware."

The room fell silent, and she stared at him with mounting hatred, which he studiously ignored. Somewhere behind the reinforced glass window, they heard the distant buzz of a security gate opening.

"It was a cover up," she said, eventually. "You doctors are all the same. You always cover for each other. My children were *ill*, and not one of those quacks knew what to do about it—"

Gregory weighed up the usefulness of fishing out the pathology reports completed in 1987 following the murders of a two-year-old boy and a girl of nine months.

Not today.

"I'm going to appeal the court ruling," she declared, though every one of her previous attempts had failed. "You know what your problem is, Doctor? You've spent so long working with crackpots, you can't tell when a sane person comes along."

She'd tried this before, too. It was a favourite pastime of hers, to try to beat the doctor at his own game. It was a classic symptom of Munchausen syndrome by proxy that the sufferer developed an obsessive interest in the medical world, and its terminology. Usually, in order to find the best way to disguise the fact they were slowly, but surely, killing their own children.

"How did it make you feel, when your husband left you, Cathy?"

Gregory nipped any forthcoming tirade neatly in the bud, and she was momentarily disarmed. Then, she gave an ugly laugh.

"Back to that old chestnut again, are we?"

When he made no reply, she ran an agitated hand through her hair.

"How would any woman feel?" she burst out. "He left me with three children, for some *tart* with cotton wool for brains. I was well rid of him."

But her index finger began to tap against the side of the chair.

Tap, tap, tap.

Tap, tap, tap.

"When was the divorce finalised, Cathy?"

"It's all there in your bloody file, isn't it?" she spat. "Why bother to ask?"

"I'm interested to know if you remember."

"Sometime in 1985," she muttered. "January, February... Emily was only a couple of months old. The bastard was at it the whole time I was pregnant."

"That must have been very hard. Why don't you tell me about it?"

Her eyes skittered about the room, all of her previous composure having evaporated.

"There's nothing to tell. He buggered off to Geneva to live in a bloody great mansion with his Barbie doll, while I was left to bring up his children. He barely even called when Emily was rushed into hospital. When *any* of them were."

"Do you think their...*illness*, would have improved, if he had?"

She gave him a sly look.

"How could it have made a difference? They were suffering from very rare conditions, outside our control."

Gregory's lips twisted, but he tried again.

"Did a part of you hope that news of their 'illness' might have encouraged your husband to return to the family home?"

"I never thought of it," she said. "All of my thoughts and prayers were spent trying to save my children."

He glanced up at the large, white plastic clock hanging on the wall above her head.

It was going to be a long morning.

An hour after Gregory finished his session with Cathy, he had just finished typing up his notes when a loud siren began to wail.

He threw open the door to his office and ran into the corridor, where the emergency alarm was louder still, echoing around the walls in a cacophony of sound. He took a quick glance in both directions and spotted a red flashing light above the doorway of one of the patients' rooms. He sprinted towards it, dimly aware of running footsteps following his own as others responded to whatever awaited them beyond the garish red light.

The heels of his shoes skidded against the floor as he reached the open doorway, where he found one of the ward nurses engaged in a mental battle with a patient who had fashioned a rudimentary knife from a sharpened fragment of metal and was presently holding it against her own neck.

Gregory reached for the alarm button and, a moment later, the wailing stopped. In the residual silence, he took a deep breath and fell back on his training.

"Do you mind if I come in?" he asked, holding out his hands, palms outstretched in the universal gesture for peace.

He exchanged a glance with the nurse, who was holding up well. He'd never ascribed to old-school hierarchies within hospital walls; doctors were no better equipped to deal with situations of this kind than an experienced mental health nurse—in fact, the reverse was often true. Life at Southmoor High Security Psychiatric Hospital followed a strict routine, for very good reason. Depending on their level of risk, patients were checked at least every fifteen minutes to try to prevent suicide attempts being made, even by those who had shown no inclination before, or who had previously been judged 'low risk'.

Especially those.

There were few certainties in the field of mental healthcare, but uncertainty was one of them.

"I'd like you to put the weapon down, Hannah," he said, calmly. "It's almost lunchtime, and it's Thursday. You know what that means."

As he'd hoped, she looked up, her grip on the knife loosening a fraction.

"Jam roly-poly day," he smiled. It was a mutual favourite of theirs and, in times of crisis, he needed to find common ground.

Anything to keep her alive.

"Sorry, Doc," she whispered, and plunged the knife into her throat.

It was a long walk back to his office, but when Gregory eventually returned some time later, he found he was not alone. A man of around fifty was seated at his desk, twirling idly on the chair while he thumbed through the most recent edition of *Psychology Today.* He wore a bobbled woollen jumper over a pair of ancient corduroy slacks, and brought with him the subtle odour of Murray Mints.

"Are you lost?"

The man looked up from the magazine and broke into a wide smile that was quickly extinguished when he spotted the bloodstains on Gregory's shirtsleeves. He rose from the desk chair and walked around to greet his protégé with open arms.

"Not all who wander are lost, m' boy."

Gregory was engulfed in a bear-like hug, which he returned, before stepping away to unbutton the shirt that clung to his skin and carried the faint, tinny odour of drying blood.

"What happened, Alex?"

"Suicide attempt by one of the regulars," he replied. "She came through."

He neglected to mention his own actions in keeping her alive, or the twenty minutes he'd spent performing CPR as the woman's blood had pumped out of her body and on to his.

It was part of the job, and nobody knew it better than the man standing before him.

Professor William Douglas was an undisputed doyen in the world of academic and clinical psychology. Thanks to his years of experience dealing with matters of the mind, he was a leading authority on abnormal and forensic psychology. He'd been the Senior Consultant Psychiatrist when Gregory had first begun his clinical training at Southmoor, more than ten years previously, and had remained a good friend and mentor ever since.

Nowadays, he spent much of his time engaged in research, having taken up a fellowship at the University of Cambridge, a cool three-hour drive away.

"What brings you here, Bill? I thought we were due to have dinner next week?"

Douglas leaned back against the edge of the desk and watched his friend root around one of his cupboards for a fresh shirt.

"I had a phone call, yesterday," he replied. "From the mayor of a small town called Ballyfinny, in County Mayo."

"Ireland?" Gregory asked, as he shrugged out of the bloodied shirt.

Douglas nodded.

"They've had some bad business, and the mayor wants someone to go over there and help to give the Garda a steer in the right direction. I can't go; I'm tied up at the university.

But I mentioned your name—"

Gregory merely shook his head.

"Profiling? We've been down that road before, Bill. We set up a special department, with photocopiers and everything, and it blew up in our faces."

He thought back to three years ago, when he'd agreed to work alongside his friend to provide scientific profiles of the perpetrators of violent crimes to police forces who asked for their help. They'd focused on cases where there were few forensic leads, or too many suspects for the police to handle with the limited resources at their disposal. The hope had been to provide a way for the police to narrow their search but, in one unforgettable case, it had helped to incarcerate an innocent man. While the police had expended time and energy prosecuting the fall-guy, the real killer of male sex workers had remained free to kill again.

And, when the shit hit the proverbial fan, their little profiling unit had been the perfect scapegoat for the public's condemning eye.

"The profiles were never supposed to be definitive," Douglas argued. "You and I both know that. We never said we could wave magic wands, or that we were clairvoyant. The profiles were created to give the police the benefit of our experience, dealing with men and women who might have committed similar crimes. There are shared traits that can help to inform their investigations—"

"You don't have to convince me," Gregory interrupted him. "I remember the work we did, and I know there were a hundred other times when we helped to save lives. It still doesn't change where we are now."

Bill Douglas ran a hand over the stubble on his chin, then decided to try a different tack.

"Before you say 'no', at least let me tell you about the case."

Gregory raised an eyebrow.

"I've got a feeling you're going to tell me, anyway."

"About a month ago, a father and daughter came home after Saturday swimming practice to find the mother dead. The little girl was the first to find her, because whoever killed Claire Kelly posed her on the kid's bed, with a teddy bear under one arm and a storybook open in her hand."

Gregory stuck his hands in his pockets and walked around his desk to stare out of the window across the lawn leading down to the perimeter fence. What kind of warped mind would set such a scene, for a little girl to find?

"Alright," he murmured. "You've got my attention."

"They have no forensic leads, no witnesses…nothing in the woman's past, no disgruntled lovers or angry ex-boyfriends. The husband's alibied to the hilt, and the whole town would give him a character reference even if he wasn't. The victim was a pillar of the community, and the police are running out of ideas—so they came to us, Alex."

"They came to *you*," his friend replied.

"Same difference," Douglas shrugged. "I'm not too proud to admit when my work's done. There isn't much more I can teach you about the human mind, and you know the door's permanently open if you want to join me at the university."

Gregory gave a small shake of his head and turned around to face him.

"There's a hell of a lot more you can teach me, and we haven't even scratched the surface of what lies out there, undiscovered."

"There might be something to learn from whoever killed that woman in Ireland." Douglas gave him a knowing smile. "You could catch a flight tomorrow and be there by lunchtime."

Gregory huffed out a laugh.

"If you can't appeal to the man, appeal to the clinician, is that it?"

Douglas was unrepentant.

"Did it work?"

Alex thought of a little girl who'd lost her mother, and of the kind of distorted mind that was responsible. The doctor inside him wanted to prevent as well as to cure, and the man…

The man just wanted to help, however he could.

"It worked," he said softly.

CHAPTER 3

Friday afternoon
County Mayo, Ireland

He was not ready to die.

This epiphany struck Gregory like a lightning bolt, as he clung to the edges of his seat inside the tiny, tin-pot aeroplane, which bounced its way through heavy storm clouds towards the landing strip at Knock Airport. He wasn't afraid of flying—never had been—but he promised himself that, if he survived this ordeal, he'd drive next time.

Or take the bus.

Hell, he'd walk, if he had to.

"Nearly there, folks," the captain's lyrical voice crackled over the tannoy. "Had a bit of turbulence back there but we'll soon have you on the ground one way or another, right enough!"

One way or another?

The plane dipped hard to the left as it began its descent, and his bowels followed with a sickening lurch.

"Makes you feel alive, doesn't it?" the man next to him called out.

Gregory gave him a queasy smile and wondered if his neighbour had been helping himself to those little bottles of booze from the trolley.

"That's one way of putting it," he said, and ordered his stomach to retain the contents of his last meal, when the plane nose-dived again.

The man laughed and gave him a slap on the back, before folding his arms and leaning back to catch a quick nap as they continued to plummet through the air.

A few moments later, he was snoring.

The plane gave another sudden jerk, and Gregory looked out of the window to check the propellers hadn't failed.

What he saw there made him catch his breath.

The plane emerged from the thick layer of cloud into glorious sunshine, which blazed trails of amber light over lush green hills and lakes glistening diamond-bright in the valley below. Like a child at the window of a sweet shop, he pressed his nose to the glass and hardly noticed the rollercoaster peaks and troughs while he soaked in the passing scenery that was Ireland's beautiful heartland.

And as the ground eventually rose up to meet the little metal bird, he was smiling.

When he stepped off the plane and onto the tarmac, Gregory felt like a new-born deer. Pride prevented him from hugging the nearest person, which happened to be an old woman of at least eighty who seemed entirely unfazed by the fact they'd recently escaped certain death. Instead, he hauled a scuffed leather weekend bag over his shoulder, grasped his briefcase, and made his way towards the low terminal building, keeping his head bowed against the driving wind that whipped across the airfield.

When he reached the arrivals area, Alex found a small welcome party waiting for him. A stocky man of indeterminate age held a card with his name written on it—which seemed superfluous given he was one of only six passengers to exit the plane—and a woman of similar build stood beside him. Both were dressed in oiled wax jackets and boots caked in mud.

"Doctor Gregory?" The woman proceeded to give him a thorough once-over.

He was a good-looking devil, that was for sure. Had a bit of the Irish about him too, if she wasn't mistaken, with his curly dark hair and green eyes. Younger than she'd imagined, but with a serious look about him that spoke of experience. Travelled light, which was no bad thing.

Once she'd completed her assessment, Alex smiled.

"Do I pass?"

The mayor of Ballyfinny pursed her lips.

"You'll do," she declared, and stuck out her hand. "Mayor Margaret Byrne. You can call me Maggie, most people do.

This here's Padraig—he works at the hotel."

"I'll take your things," the man said, and slid the bag from Gregory's shoulder before he could protest.

"It was good of you to meet me," Gregory said, as they followed Padraig's loping gait towards the exit. "I'd have been happy to get a taxi."

"Hard to come by, on Fridays. All the young ones book them up for a night out in Galway. We're near the county border here," she added.

"I was sorry to hear of the trouble you've had." he said quietly. "I don't know if I can help you, but I'm willing to try."

The mayor paused beneath the canopy outside the terminal and heaved a sigh as she watched people coming and going, raising an occasional hand to those who passed by.

"Some say I did the wrong thing, calling Bill Douglas, inviting you over here to meddle in our affairs," she said, forthrightly. "You should know that, from the get-go. People in these parts are hurting, and, as for the local Garda, they want to be the ones to bring in whoever's responsible for taking Claire Kelly away from her family. Last thing they need is an outsider—an *English* outsider—coming over to tell them how to do their jobs."

"I don't intend to do that."

She nodded.

"Just as well. Ballyfinny might be a small town, but we're no hillbillies. My boys trained over at the Garda College in Templemore—and the NBCI in Dublin—before they came back home to Mayo."

She referred to the Garda National Bureau of Criminal Investigation, headquartered in Dublin, whose detectives were responsible for investigating serious and organised crimes in Ireland.

"Your boys?" he asked.

"My sons," she told him, with a touch of pride. "They're both with the Divisional Garda, and they've been working the case. You should know that, too."

Small towns, Gregory thought. Everybody knew everybody else, which was something that could help them to catch Claire Kelly's killer.

"Seems like you had a lot of opposition," he said. "It's not too late to change your mind."

Maggie gave him a considering look.

"You've got a quiet thread of steel in you," she observed. "You'll need it."

With that, she jutted her chin towards a battered-looking Land Rover, where Padraig was leaning against the driver's door puffing his way through a rollie.

"Come on, lad. You must be ready for a good meal."

"I ate on the plane."

She smiled.

"Like I said, you must be ready for a good meal."

CHAPTER 4

There was little conversation as the Land Rover ambled its way off the beaten track and into the wilds of County Mayo, following winding, single-track lanes past hills and glades on the picturesque journey from Knock Airport to Ballyfinny. Gregory watched the passing hamlets and villages, noting the ancient churches and quaint, white-painted cottages Ireland was famous for and thought that, had the circumstances been different, he would've liked to spend more time exploring its treasures.

"Hotel's up here on the left," Maggie said. "It's the only one around these parts—also happens to be the best."

"That's a happy coincidence," he replied, and made her smile.

"I should know," she said. "My brother manages the place."

Small towns, Gregory thought again. He'd need to be careful what he said, and to whom.

The Land Rover braked sharply and made a left turn through a set of imposing, pillared gates onto a thick, forested driveway. The trees were old and had grown tall, blotting out most of the natural light as they followed the road leading to the main entrance of the Ballyfinny Castle Hotel. There was a stillness to the forest, Gregory thought, as they drove further beneath its canopy.

And darkness that could conceal all manner of sins.

Presently, they emerged from the trees back into the light, and Padraig slowed the car as the road forked. To the left, an impressive, crenelated castle perched atop a gentle hill, its manicured lawns falling away to the banks of an enormous lough which glimmered in the late afternoon sun.

"Where does the other road lead?" Gregory asked.

"To the town," Maggie replied. "You can walk there in ten minutes, if you've a mind to. Folk have their houses all the way around the waterside, dotted here and there. Some have their own boats."

"Where was Claire Kelly's house?"

The mood in the car shifted, and Padraig's spine stiffened behind the wheel.

"About five minutes further along that road," Maggie replied. "The Kelly house is on the edge of town. Somebody will take you there, if you want to see it."

Gregory wanted to get a feel for the place straight away, eager as he was to get started, but he knew things didn't work that way. There were hoops to step through, first.

"Took the liberty of inviting my boys to come and meet

you over dinner," Maggie continued. "Thought it'd be good for you all to…get acquainted."

Under the watchful eye of their mother, he surmised.

In his experience, the police had their own ways of doing things. Those ways seldom responded well to outside interference; but then, he hadn't accounted for that interference coming in the form of the town mayor, who also happened to be the mother of two of the town's finest boys in blue.

The car rattled up the remainder of the sweeping driveway and came to a shuddering standstill outside the main entrance to the hotel.

"We're here," Padraig said, and slammed out of the car.

Aideen McArdle hummed as she unpegged laundry from the line outside the cottage she'd lived in for over forty years. It wasn't much, she supposed, not by some standards. But, to her, it was her sanctuary, the home she had worked hard to build. Every floor and wall held a lifetime of memories, both good and bad.

Mostly, good.

"I'll be off now, then, my love."

Her husband stuck his head out of the kitchen door and blew her a kiss.

"Don't think you can sweet-talk me, Colm McArdle. You'd best be back here before eleven or, so help me, there'll be a holy show in this house."

He threw a hand to his heart.

"In the name of God, woman! When have I ever been out so late?" he asked, with every appearance of sincerity.

She dragged a sheet off the line with exaggerated force.

"Only every given Saturday," she muttered, and pointed a warning finger. "Mind yourself, Colm. You're not as young as you used to be."

"Now, she insults me!" he proclaimed, to nobody in particular. "I'm as able as any man to share a pint of the black stuff with me pals and stumble home afterwards."

"More able than most," she mumbled, with a peg between her lips.

Her husband trotted up the garden path and slipped his arms around her waist, chuckling when she yelped in surprise and tried to bat him away.

"Give us a kiss, colleen," he murmured, as he'd done all those years ago.

Aideen smiled to herself, and favoured him with a quick peck.

"There's more of that, if you get yourself home in one piece."

She was still smiling as he made his way back inside the house, whistling an old tune between his teeth. It was a fine life they led, all told. It had been hard in the early years, it was true, but what young couple didn't have their share of problems to iron out? They'd made the best of it, and of themselves—and were happy now because of it.

With creaking knees, she bent to retrieve the laundry basket. These simple tasks weren't as easy as they used to be, but she was damned if she'd get a cleaner in to help.

She'd sooner go to the glue factory.

Aideen nudged the back door closed with her hip and went about the rest of her day, never thinking anybody had seen their private exchange; never suspecting the lengths one person had gone to, just to spend the time watching her, admiring her.

Loving her.

They made a careful note of the time Colm McArdle left the house, and smiled. That made four weeks in a row he'd left around five-thirty. The daylight was fading fast, but in another week or two, it would have disappeared entirely as the long, winter nights set in.

It'd be very soon, now.

After a quick shower and change, Alexander Gregory retraced his steps through the grand hallways of the Ballyfinny Castle Hotel. It was an imposing, thirteenth-century edifice, which had been home to one of Ireland's oldest and wealthiest families. As such, it boasted hundreds of priceless artefacts and antiques, gleaming silverware and chandeliers in every room—including the gents—and was precisely the opposite of the faded Bed and Breakfast he had expected to find in a small, backwater town.

But, when he reached the bottom of the main flight of stairs, he was reminded of why Ballyfinny would never be a 'backwater'. A long bank of windows looked out across the lough, which gleamed like burnished gold in the setting sun. The little ferry that carried passengers to various stopping points around the water chugged slowly back towards the hotel jetty, like something from a picture postcard. Thick pine trees grew right up to the water's edge and were reflected in the rippling water that lapped against the shore.

Views like that would always attract visitors; people who came from far and wide to enjoy the kind of tranquillity they lacked in their ordinary lives.

People like him, he thought.

The hotel had recently been taken over by some international conglomerate or another, who'd apparently had the good sense and foresight to appoint a local person to run the place on its behalf. That duty fell to Maggie's brother; a tall, stately gentleman with a belly like Father Christmas, who awaited him now in the reception area.

"Doctor Gregory? I'm Seamus Murphy, General Manager of the hotel."

Gregory took his hand, and found it firm.

"Thanks for putting me up at short notice," he replied. "You've got a beautiful spot, here."

"Aye, and we're hoping it won't be tarnished by all that's happened," Seamus replied, earning himself a reproachful glare from his sister, who hovered beside him. "It's an awful thing, Maggie, but it's only the truth. We've had over twenty cancellations since word got out about what happened to Claire Kelly, and I've got a hotel full of staff to think of—all with bills to pay and young mouths to feed."

"That may be so, but it's hardly the time to think of such a thing," she snapped, then turned to Gregory in mild embarrassment. "As you can see, this murder has had an effect on all of us. I've got more'n half the town breathing down my neck, calling for justice. Liam Kelly calls my office most mornings, begging to know whether anything's being done. On the other side, the police are doing all they can, with what they can. I'm at my wit's end."

"I understand," Alex replied, diplomatically. "It's in everybody's interest to see her killer brought to justice as soon as possible."

Maggie made a sound like a *harrumph,* and he smiled. He found that he liked this woman with her mop of wild grey hair and no-nonsense attitude. It was refreshing to find someone apparently so unaffected by public office.

But then, appearances were often deceptive.

"Sorry we're late, Ma. Some daft bugger in a rented Mercedes drove straight into the back of Ned Malloy's tractor—"

Gregory turned to see two men of around his own age cross the hotel foyer. At first glance, they were indistinguishable, both being of above-average height, with dark brown hair and eyes. Upon closer inspection, he noticed one was slightly taller and broader than the other, who had a lean, wiry build.

"Never mind—you're here now," Maggie replied. "Doctor Alexander Gregory, meet my eldest son, Detective Inspector Niall Byrne, who heads up the Divisional Garda office over in Castlebar," she said, indicating the stockier of the two. "And this here's my youngest, Sergeant Connor Byrne, who heads up the local Garda office right here in Ballyfinny."

Both men donned polite smiles, which Gregory assumed to be exclusively for their mother's benefit.

"Glad to meet you," he said, and wondered whether the difference in rank had caused any sibling rivalry over the years.

Hazard of the job.

"So, I hear you're some sort of head doctor," Niall said, sticking his hands in the pockets of his trousers. "Come all this way to read our minds? Why don't you tell me what I'm thinking right now?"

Maggie flushed an angry shade of red and opened her mouth to intervene, but Gregory beat her to it.

"You're thinking what we're all thinking, inspector," he said, easily. "Murder, and dinner. Not necessarily in that order."

There was a second's pause, and then Niall Byrne laughed shortly.

"Let's at least get the dinner part out of the way, first."

CHAPTER 5

Seamus Murphy flexed some of his managerial muscle to secure a private dining room, away from prying eyes inside the main restaurant. None of their party was naïve enough to imagine that word had not already spread about Gregory's arrival but, with tensions already running high, there was no need to broadcast the fact. Speculation was the bane of any detective's existence, even the well-meaning kind, and there had been plenty of that already.

Soon enough, they were seated at a gleaming mahogany table inside a small side room, with mullioned windows overlooking the forest. As the sun made its final descent on the far horizon, the temperature outside dropped. Mist rolled in from the water and curled its way through the tree trunks like long fingers, twisting a pathway through the woods before disappearing into the penetrating darkness.

"So, doctor, you're here to tell us we're looking for a white male, aged eighteen to forty-five. Am I right?"

As the senior-ranking officer in the room, Niall Byrne seemed to have taken it upon himself to lead the discussion and, if Gregory was not mistaken, the general tone.

"I'll thank you to remember that Doctor Gregory is here as our *guest*," his mother hissed, but Niall merely shrugged.

"I'm sure Doctor Gregory's time is precious, and he doesn't want to waste it on a fool's errand," he replied, and fixed him with a challenging stare. "I don't rightly know what a criminal profiler can possibly do to help us, Ma. Not when half the Garda of County Mayo have already tried… unless he feels he's better qualified than any of us?"

Gregory had heard the tone countless times before, in and out of his consulting room, and prepared himself for a battle.

"What Niall means to say is—" Maggie began.

"Detective Inspector Byrne means to say, 'What the hell is a stranger doing coming over here, trying to tell me how to do my job?' " he interjected, mildly.

Niall inclined his head.

"Nothing wrong with your ears, Doc."

"Give the feller a chance," his brother murmured, from the chair beside him. "He isn't the one we're lookin' for."

Niall folded his arms across his burly chest.

"We can look after our *own*," he growled.

"There's Liam Kelly to think of, and his wee girl," Maggie said. "You've gone over and over it but there's nothing new. It's time for a fresh pair of eyes."

Gregory wasn't sure whether her authority was derived from her status as their mother, or as the mayor of the town but, either way, both men fell silent.

He took that as his cue.

"Let's get a few things straight," he said. "I'm a senior psychologist at Southmoor Hospital, in London. It's a high-security facility, and I work exclusively with people who've been legally detained by the courts, either because they're a serious danger to themselves or to others. Usually, both."

"You try to cure them," Niall surmised, and his lip curled.

Rocky ground, Gregory thought. And the retribution-reform debate was something they had no time for, at present.

"You need a shield *and* a sword for balance in this world," he ventured to say. "But, let's not get into that now. What you need to know is that I've seen a lot of very unstable people, who've committed terrible crimes, like the one committed against Claire Kelly. Every patient is different, they've come from a range of backgrounds but, nonetheless, I've seen certain…*similarities*. There are patterns that might help to paint a picture of the sort of person you're looking for. Maybe you'll recognise something—"

"They're not all mad," Seamus interrupted, causing four heads to turn in his direction. "I read about the Yorkshire Ripper, who had all the psychologists fooled for a while back in the eighties. Told everyone it was the 'voices' that made him do it, but that was a load of old blarney. Who's to say all these 'unstable' people aren't just playing the system?"

Gregory nodded.

"I agree," he said, surprising them all. "Not every person who kills or commits violent crime is legally insane, but that doesn't mean they're fine and dandy, either. Look, I won't tell you the system is perfect, because it isn't. We just try to do the best we can with it."

He paused, watching Seamus break his bread roll into six perfectly even pieces.

"I try to help the perpetrators, but that doesn't mean I've forgotten the victims. I never forget the people who've been on the receiving end and, if you're worrying that I'll be looking to provide whoever killed Claire Kelly with some kind of psychological excuse for his—or *her*—actions, you're mistaken. Questions of culpability are for the police and the courts to decide."

Conversation paused while the door re-opened to admit their waiter, only resuming after it closed again.

"What do you get out of it?" Connor asked, quietly.

Gregory turned to face the younger of the Byrne brothers.

"Same as you," he said eventually. "I get to know that, in the end, there'll be one less of them roaming the streets. Some of them are compulsive, some of them are careful planners. But, in the end, they're killers—and they need to be stopped."

For the first time that evening, a broad smile broke across Niall's face.

"Well, why the heck didn't you say so in the first place?" he asked.

CHAPTER 6

The discussion did not turn to Claire Kelly's murder until the plates had been cleared, for which Alex could only be grateful. He had a strong constitution, and the sight of blood alone did not unsettle him, nor did crime scene photographs—they were enough to turn any man's stomach, but they were merely evidence of something far greater and more disturbing.

The outer limits of the human mind.

In keeping with Garda protocols, Seamus Murphy and Mayor Byrne excused themselves from the table, the latter pausing to put a motherly hand on his shoulder.

"Despite the frosty welcome," she said, throwing one last disapproving glance towards her sons, "I want to say that I'm grateful you're here, Alex. Even if there's only the remotest possibility something'll come of it, we have to try."

She turned an imperious cheek in his direction and Gregory realised it was an invitation to give her a peck goodnight.

After a moment's hesitation, he did.

Afterwards, Maggie moved around the room, fussing over her boys and reminding them to get some sleep as she bade them a lengthy farewell. Gregory watched the ritual, which was one he'd observed many times before. Unbidden, an image of Cathy Jones popped into his mind. He thought of all the cloying attention she'd given her children—even singing a lullaby as she'd spooned salt into her baby's bottle.

Was it any wonder that some people grew up to be killers?

The door closed and, in the ensuing silence, Niall and Connor Byrne loosened their ties in one synchronised motion and reached for the bottle of wine sitting half-full on the table.

All cop, now, Gregory thought.

"Look, you seem like a decent bloke," Niall said, topping off his glass. "It was nothing personal, before—"

"Not at all."

"It's just that we get a lot of charlatans calling in, telling us they've seen the ghost of Claire Kelly and all that," Connor explained. "Had somebody calling herself Mystic Mandy ring the station the other day, would you believe."

"It's not just the local crazies, either," Niall put in, and shot Gregory an apologetic look. "No offence, Doc, but I say it as I see it. We've had 'em calling in from all over this blessed island, claiming to be her killer."

"Any of them seem genuine?" Gregory asked, but both brothers shook their heads.

"We followed up on all of them," Niall said. "But none could tell us exactly where, or how, Claire Kelly was found. That's not public knowledge," he added.

Your mother knows, Gregory almost said, *and so does Padraig.*

"I heard she was found on the little girl's bed," he said instead. "Staged with a book, and a teddy?"

Niall ran a tired hand over his face.

"Aye, she was found like that," he said, and turned to his brother. "Connor was the first on-scene, after the family."

"Took a call from her husband," Connor said quietly. "When I got to the house, he was just sitting on the front lawn outside, rocking little Emily back and forth. Never seen a man more broken in all my life."

He sucked in a deep breath before continuing.

"I couldn't get much sense out of him then, not when the little one was there to hear, so I took a look inside the house. Didn't take much looking, before I found her."

The little girl was called Emily, Gregory thought. *Just like Cathy Jones' baby daughter.*

Annoyed at himself, he shoved the thought of his patient to one side and told himself to focus on the matters in hand.

"How did Claire die?" he asked, after a heavy silence.

"Single knife wound to the heart," Connor replied. "Doctor arrived pretty quick, but anybody could see she was gone."

"There must have been blood everywhere," Gregory thought aloud, and grieved all over again for the child and what she must have seen.

But Niall shook his head.

"Whoever it is, he took his time. Bastard whacked Claire around the head, first, to immobilise her. Then, far as we can

40

tell, he took her into the bathroom and put her in the tub. That's where he used the knife and let her bleed out nice and tidy. Washed her up, afterwards, put duct tape over the knife wound, then dressed her up like a doll and took her through to Emily's bedroom."

Gregory was silent for a full minute, then he rose from the table and moved to the window to stare unseeingly at the night sky.

"What about the knife?" he asked. "What was used to immobilise her?"

"Single blow to the back of the head," Connor replied. "They used the back of a bronze sculpture from the hallway table—"

"Which he cleaned, thoroughly," Niall put in. "We only found out it was used after the forensics team came in. Even then, there was barely a spot of blood left on it. Same story with the bathtub; we only found out it was the kill site after they examined the pipes. Everything else was spotless."

"Meticulous," Gregory muttered. "And he gained access into the house."

"As for the knife, we haven't found it," Connor went on. "We've examined everything that fits the bill at the Kelly home, but the lab work came back clean. He must have taken it away with him."

"We've been scouring the area," Niall said. "No sign of it, yet."

The killing had elements of ritual, Gregory thought, *which necessitated a special implement in the mind of the one who had performed it. Not just any knife would do.*

"What about DNA or prints?" he asked. "Must've been something on the duct tape."

"Only as you'd expect," Niall replied, unable to hide his frustration. "Plenty of samples from Liam and Claire, old prints from the wider family and a few from the first responders, but not a single other alien print or sample. No sexual assault—no semen, either."

Small mercy, Gregory thought, but it didn't mean her killer hadn't enjoyed himself.

"What about the victim's life? Was there anyone troubling Claire Kelly before she died?"

"Nobody," Connor replied. "She had a clean bill of health, no skeletons rattling around in her closet."

"We've knocked on doors, checked all the CCTV, and spoken to everybody in a five-mile radius, but it's like the bastard disappeared into thin air," Niall said. "Nobody saw a damn thing."

"Had to be an outsider," Connor decided, while Gregory was lost in his own thoughts. "Nobody in Ballyfinny would do something so…so *evil.*"

"It's probably some lunatic over from the city, just wandered into the first house he came to," Niall agreed. "We've a small community here, and none of them could've done this."

Gregory turned to him with solemn eyes.

"I'm afraid I disagree with you," he said. "An outsider could never have known how to perfectly time the attack for when Claire Kelly was likely to be alone in the house—long enough for him to set the scene he had in mind."

"Could've got lucky," Connor argued.

"Or, they might have been monitoring her routines. In my experience, violent attacks like these come after weeks or months of planning, where the perpetrator stalks their victim first, building up to the final act," Gregory said. "The preparation, the careful execution, it all speaks of experience. This won't be the first time."

"We've never had anything like this happen here before," Niall said. "It must be an outsider."

Once again, Gregory shook his head.

"When I say it isn't their 'first time', I don't mean they've killed in the same way before. I mean they might have been cautioned for other, milder offences. They might have killed or hurt animals. Have you had any Peeping Toms?"

"There've been a couple," Niall acknowledged. "But, to go from that, to what happened to Claire…it's a big leap."

"Not in their mind," Gregory said. "They might've been building up to it for years."

Connor scrubbed a hand over the back of his neck and appealed to his elder brother.

"I still can't believe it's one of our own."

"I don't want to, Con, but I can't help but see the sense of it," Niall murmured. "And, if Alex is right, if it's one of ours who's been working up to killing—"

He looked over at the tall, sombre man standing beside the window, who simply nodded.

"There's every chance they'll kill again," Gregory said. "They've managed to get away with murder for over a month.

They'll be feeling invincible, but the rush will be fading. The urge to kill again will be strong."

"How do we stop them?" Niall shot back. "How the *hell* do we stop them, if we don't know where to look?"

"We look at the victim," Gregory said simply. "We ask ourselves: 'What it was about Claire Kelly that was so special?' Why her, and why in that way?"

"Not just her," Connor said, and Niall swore beneath his breath. "She was two months pregnant when she died."

The breath lodged somewhere in Gregory's chest, and he let it out again, very slowly.

"That's another angle to consider," he said, once his emotions were back in check. "And it means we have a double murderer on our hands."

Another thought struck him.

"It's common for a killer to seek to…*recapture* the rush, by visiting their victim's grave site. Have you kept the cemetery under surveillance?"

The two Garda detectives looked amongst themselves, then Niall leaned forward.

"I thought somebody would have told you," he said. "Claire's body was only released a few days ago. The funeral's tomorrow morning."

"We're drafting in more guards to manage the crowds," Connor added. "The whole town's likely to be there, and more besides."

Yes, Gregory thought. *Much more besides.*

With an entire township there to mourn his handiwork, how could the killer resist?

He turned back to the window, listening to the dim sound of merriment wafting through the walls of the restaurant next door. They were out there, somewhere, he thought. Walking and talking, just like everybody else.

But inside…

Inside was a festering mass; a rotten core that must be cut out, before it was too late.

CHAPTER 7

Saturday

The woods smelled earthy and sweet, like the over-ripe scent of death.

The trees were dense, packed so tightly their branches had knitted together, obliterating the moon which shone somewhere in the heavens above. Thin leaves brushed his face as Alex wound his way between them, his feet crunching the soft ground underfoot as he followed the blurry light flickering in the darkness up ahead. His hands reached blindly into the night, feeling his way through the forest as he tried to touch it. He heard his own breath, impossibly loud in the surrounding silence, and the thunder of blood as it pumped through his veins.

The light grew brighter, and his pace quickened, his feet tripping over pine cones as he hurried forward.

Unexpectedly, he stumbled into a clearing.

For a moment, the moonlight blinded him. He threw up a hand to shield his eyes against its glare, then let it fall away again when he heard the faint sound of a baby's cry.

In the centre of the clearing, a woman was seated on a child's bed, bathed in a halo of light. Her skin was deathly white, her fingers bloodless as they clutched a small teddy bear against her chest.

"You're too late," she whispered.

He tried to rush forward, but found he couldn't move. His limbs were suspended, as though he was trapped inside a glass cage, unable to break free.

In his hotel bed, Alexander Gregory began to thrash against the sheets, his body rearing up from the pillows.

Across the clearing, another figure stepped out of the shadows. She smiled at them both, her eyes vividly alive, her painted mouth a slash of blood-red.

"I'll take care of the child," she crooned. "I take good care of *all* my children."

The baby's cry grew louder then, echoing around the clearing. It grew louder and more desperate until he sank to his knees, pressing the heels of his hands against his ears to try to drown out the phantom sound.

"You're too late," Cathy Jones said, and took a seat beside Claire Kelly amongst the soft toys. He watched the dead woman turn glassy eyes towards his patient, then hand over the teddy bear for safekeeping.

No!

He screamed the word in his mind, clawing his way free from the covers on his bed.

No! Don't give it to her!

Claire Kelly turned towards him, and in the centre of her chest, there was a gaping wound where her heart ought to have been.

Alex awoke with a shout, shaking and disoriented.

His body was covered in a film of clammy sweat, the bedclothes tangled at his feet. His heart raced as adrenaline rushed through his system, preparing him to stay and fight, or cut and run. He'd left a light burning beside the bed, and it shone a comforting glow around the hotel room. He leaned back against the antique headboard and concentrated on taking slow, even breaths while he thought of a quote from Gandhi that Bill Douglas had once told him, at the end of a particularly bad day at the hospital:

Each night, when I go to sleep, I die. And the next morning, when I wake up, I am reborn.

The constriction in his chest began to ease, and Alex looked around the room as if he was seeing it for the first time. He didn't need to be a psychologist to understand the meaning of his dream, or what his own psyche was trying to tell him.

He was an impostor.

Who was he to think he could help the Garda—he, the 'criminal profiler', who was nothing more than a shrink? He was an interloper, a stranger to these shores, unqualified to pronounce judgment on its people, or its community. It wasn't his job to hunt killers—it was his job to treat them.

When the police eventually tracked them down.

Alex swung his legs off the bed and padded into the adjoining bathroom, where he ran the cold tap and splashed water over his face and neck—once, twice, three times.

Then he leaned on the countertop and took a good look at the man who stared back.

His hair was dishevelled and flecked with the first hint of grey at the temples. His skin was drawn tightly across a symmetrical face, where everything fitted together with the kind of harmony people seemed to admire. It was a deceptively youthful face, despite the fine laughter lines around the eyes and mouth. Quick to laugh, quick to smile.

But it was the eyes that gave him away.

They were a deep, arresting shade of green, and fathoms deep with sadness; the kind that came from delving into the hearts and souls of those wracked in torment. A little rubbed off each time, though he tried to prevent it. A shadow of their fear and self-loathing imprinted itself on his memory and made a home there, swirling around the cavern of his mind until he could no longer tell where they ended, and Alexander Gregory began.

He turned away and walked to the bedroom window, where he pulled back the curtains. Outside, a new day was preparing to dawn, and the lough was a melting pool of deep lilac-blue. He watched birds of prey swoop down over the water and rise up again with triumphant cries, and was forcibly reminded of his purpose in being there.

His eyes strayed across to a thick cardboard file resting on the desk nearby. It contained summary notes, reports and images pertaining to the murder of Claire Kelly, and he'd read it cover to cover the night before. Somewhere within that file lay the answer to why she had been chosen; why, of all the women in the town, she had been so unlucky.

Or, so special.

With one last, lingering look at the rising sun, he prepared to delve into the shadows once more.

CHAPTER 8

Gregory walked a full circuit of the castle grounds before following the road that led to Ballyfinny. People emerged from scattered cottages along the way, wearing dark clothing and mournful expressions. They greeted him with mild suspicion, but their footsteps formed a procession and they followed the winding country lane through the trees and over tiny, hump-backed bridges until they reached the town centre.

As Connor Byrne had predicted, the whole town had turned out for Claire Kelly's funeral.

Ballyfinny was quintessentially Irish; a small, stone-built haven with an enormous abbey church far too big for the population thereabouts, a white-washed pub by the name of 'O'Feeney's', and any number of tea rooms set back from the cobble-stoned streets that were presently swollen with people in varying shades of black, grey and navy blue.

Gregory melted into the crowd, his eyes tracking the faces of those he passed, searching for a sign or, perhaps, a miracle…

The breath was suddenly knocked from his body, and he braced two hands against the child who ran headlong into his stomach.

He found himself looking down at the flushed face of a boy of five or six.

"Watch where you're going, Mister," he said, and would have run off again but for the staying hand that came to rest on his shoulder.

"I'm so sorry," his mother said, as she caught up with her wayward son. "Declan's a ball of energy at the moment and doesn't always watch where he's going. I hope he didn't hurt you."

"No harm done," Gregory said, and smiled at the gap-toothed child between them. "How about you, kiddo?"

"I'm thirsty," he declared.

His mother produced a bottle of water from her bag, which he proceeded to chug down like a desert camel.

"Mammy," the boy said, once he'd come up for air. "There's Sophie and Finn!"

"Alright," she murmured. "You go on ahead, I'll catch up."

The boy bolted off in search of his friends, who waved to him from the steps of the abbey.

"You're not from around here," the woman said, turning back to Gregory. "Were you a friend of Claire's?"

Alex shook his head, and wondered how much to say.

"I'm a friend of the Mayor," he replied. "I'm here to pay my respects."

"You must be the psychologist."

"Is it so obvious?"

A gust of wind caught the woman's hair, lifting it away from her face to reveal a porcelain complexion, dusted with freckles. He scarcely had time to admire them, before the wind changed again.

"You've a serious, watchful look about you," she admitted. "But it isn't that. You're the only Englishman in town."

He nodded sagely.

"That narrows it down, a bit."

"We'd better go inside," she said, but made no move to leave.

He recognised the feeling. She wanted to prolong their exchange, just as he did, because there was chemistry here.

Unfortunately, it was something neither of them wanted to explore.

"I worked with Claire at the school," she told him, and couldn't keep the emotion from her voice. "She was a good friend."

"I'm sorry," he said. There were no other, better words.

"D'you think you can help?"

Gregory was an honest man in most things, and he gave an honest answer to the woman with windswept red hair.

"I'm going to try."

She nodded, and heaved her bag higher on her shoulder, preparing to join her family.

"I'll be seeing you," she said.

"What's your name?" he asked, reaching out a hand to brush her arm.

"Emma," she said.

A moment later, she was gone.

Gregory watched her disappear into the crowd, then followed at a slower pace, keeping time with the *clip-clop* sound of hooves belonging to the traditional carriage hearse somewhere up ahead. The scene made him think of a biblical Exodus in reverse, with hundreds of people making their way to the church in eerie silence. Most of them moved in family clusters, others in couples, but rarely did he see anybody travelling alone. There were no loners skulking conveniently beside the church walls, nor any wild-eyed men or women who stood out from their neighbours.

The town moved together, united in its outpouring of grief.

And yet, a predator roamed freely amongst them, undetected and unstoppable, at least in their own mind—which was the most dangerous place of all.

Inside the abbey, it was standing room only.

At the foot of the altar, a priest stood resplendent in golden robes, his face suitably downcast as he exchanged a word with Maggie, who was dressed in a black trouser suit and sensible heels, looking every inch the town mayor. Her face was stoical; an emotion demanded of those in positions of authority, especially at moments such as these. On the front row, a small girl of three or four was seated beside her grandparents, two dark pigtails just visible over the back of the wooden pew. The Garda had turned out in force. Connor and Niall Byrne wore full dress uniform, as did the guards who were stationed by the perimeter walls.

Gregory positioned himself at the back nearest the door, which afforded a clear view of proceedings and, more importantly, would allow him to observe anyone who slipped in or out before the funeral was over. Following their discussion, measures had been taken to ensure the doors remained under surveillance, but it was easy to miss somebody amid the throng.

When the priest moved to the head of the central aisle, an instant hush spread throughout the congregation. The local boys' choir began to sing the first bars of a requiem and, though he could not claim any religious affiliation, Gregory was moved by its rousing melody, which resonated around the church walls.

Heads turned as Claire Kelly's husband began his slow, painful journey down the central aisle, flanked by five other men who held her coffin aloft. When Gregory caught sight of the man's face as he gripped the edges of the polished wood, he saw only raw, naked grief; the kind that could rarely be feigned.

Flowers fell as the coffin travelled onward and, while the townsfolk sent up prayers for the man and his child, one of their number scanned the pews, seeking another face.

The next face.

Aideen.

CHAPTER 9

"Might've known it'd be you."

Alex stumbled across the mayor in a far corner of the churchyard, where she had stationed herself behind the wide girth of a tree to puff on an e-cigarette while she stared out across the gravestones and enjoyed a moment away from the madding crowd.

"I can leave," he offered.

"It'd do no good," she said, and let out a long stream of smoke. "No matter which way I turn, there's still a girl of three without her mother, and not a bloody thing I can do about it."

Gregory tucked his hands into his pockets.

At the family's request, Maggie had given Claire Kelly's eulogy less than an hour before. Though she wasted few words on small talk, her eloquence at the lectern had given him new insight into her character. Her voice rang out clearly and hadn't faltered, though much of the congregation had been reduced to tears.

But now, the effort had drained her, and she looked all of her sixty-three years in the unforgiving light of the midday sun.

"You gave an excellent speech," he said.

She took another drag of the minty smoke, then looked down at the canister with distaste.

"Times like these, this muck just doesn't cut it," she muttered, and heaved a sigh. "You know what I was thinking about, while I was up there, Alex?"

He waited.

"I was thinking about the fact *he* might be sitting there, in one of the pews, revelling in it all," she spat, waving away the question he hadn't bothered to ask. "Niall told me about your theory that it's one of our own, and that he wouldn't miss the chance to come to the funeral."

"It might not be a 'he," Gregory corrected, and she looked shocked.

"I can't believe it."

"The act itself, or the fact a woman might have committed it?" he asked.

"Both."

He wasn't surprised. Most people couldn't bring themselves to imagine it, particularly of the 'fairer' sex.

"At Southmoor, I work primarily with women," he explained. "Although violent crimes tend to be perpetrated by men, believe me, some women are just as capable. I meet them every day."

Maggie rubbed a hand over her temple to ease the pounding headache that was presently drilling a hole in her skull.

"Nobody in the town has a history of anything like this," she said. "I made it my business to know. Connor and Niall ran a check on every person in the neighbourhood."

"They might not have a history of murder," Gregory said. "But they do now."

She swore, then tugged a rosary from her pocket and kissed it quickly, before she was condemned to hell and damnation.

"What I want to know is *why*," she said. "That woman never harmed a soul in her life."

Gregory moved to lean back against the tree trunk beside her, settling his long body beside hers.

"Why kill anyone?" he was bound to say. "But, in this instance, I think the killer saw something in Claire that triggered their innermost need."

"Need? For what?"

"I don't know, yet. I need to understand who Claire was," he explained. "At times like these, it's natural to focus on her killer, to imagine them as all kinds of monster, but the fact is they look just like you or me. The key to finding her killer is to look at Claire and understand what she represented to them."

"Con and Niall have tried," she said. "They've looked at her life every which way."

Gregory gave a small shake of his head, trying to find the words to explain.

"It isn't so much what she did in her life; whether she worked as a teacher, whether she had friends and so forth. It's what it all adds up to; the *substance* of the woman, and how she appeared to others."

"She was *normal*," Maggie muttered.

"There's an interesting word," he replied. "I haven't met many 'normal' people. Perhaps that's what set her apart."

Maggie looked past him, across the cemetery.

"There's one person who knows the innermost thoughts of the folk around here," she said, and nodded towards the priest, whose long robes brushed against the grass as he made his way to the vestry door. "It's a good place to start."

The abbey was almost deserted by the time Gregory ducked back inside. Without hundreds of warm bodies lining its pews, the air was cool and whistled through the cracks in the old stone walls. Autumn sunshine filtered through ornate stained-glass windows lining either side of the nave, but the rainbow colours did little to relieve the oppressive atmosphere and his eye was drawn to an enormous golden crucifix suspended above the altar. The weeping effigy of Christ had loomed over Claire Kelly's coffin during her funeral, and he was reminded of one of his early sessions with Cathy Jones.

"Is religion important to you, Cathy?" he'd asked.

"Of course, Doctor. I almost lost my faith, after Emily was taken from me. When Christopher was taken as well, I couldn't imagine why a benevolent god would let my sweet babies die."

The salt might have had something to do with it, he'd thought. *Or the malnourishment and chronic sleep deprivation.* Inducing illness was a classic symptom of factitious disorder imposed on another, more commonly known as Munchausen syndrome by proxy.

"I found my faith again and I pray each night that you and the other doctors will come to your senses. When I was at home, I used to have a crucifix on my bedside table. Do you think they'd let me have it back?"

Gregory thought of his patient back at Southmoor, praying fervently to whichever god would listen. Her disordered mind was convinced her bereavement had been an act of divinity, but he wondered what Claire Kelly's killer had thought as they stood inside the hallowed walls of God's house.

Had they prayed for forgiveness, or had their sins already been absolved?

Did they believe they were on a divine mission, or one entirely of their own making?

From the shadowed cloisters, the priest watched the play of emotions on his face and wondered if he knew how much he wore on his sleeve.

"Doctor Gregory, isn't it?"

The mask slipped back into place and Alex turned with a smile to greet the priest of Ballyfinny.

"Father Walsh?"

"Sean."

He shook hands with a man of average height, with a smooth, rounded face and mild brown eyes. During the funeral service, the priest had seemed much taller—bedecked in golden robes and with the weight of two thousand years of Catholic dogma behind him, rather than the plain black cassock and clerical collar he now wore.

"Maggie said you wanted to speak to me about Claire."

"If it isn't an inconvenient moment, Father."

Walsh shook his head and indicated a carved oak door.

"Let's make ourselves comfortable," he said. "It's been a hard morning, and I'm sure we could both use a cup of tea."

Gregory followed the man to a side door, consciously slowing his footsteps to match the priest's slower pace. At Southmoor, the next crisis was never far away, and he'd developed a habit of covering the ground quickly. But here, in this rural corner of the world, the pace of life was much slower.

It took some adjustment.

"Did you know Mrs Kelly well, before she died?" he asked, ducking his head inside a small doorway leading to the priest's study.

"As well as any of my congregation," Walsh replied, making his way across the room to a kitchen area, where he set a kettle to boil. "I knew Claire to be a regular churchgoer, who came to Mass every week with her family. I took up the position here in Ballyfinny two years ago, after Father

Quinion passed, so I'm afraid I missed little Emily Kelly's baptism and the Kellys' wedding."

He plopped a couple of tea bags into mismatching cups, while Gregory looked on.

"Where were you before?" he asked.

"Here, there, and roundabouts," the priest smiled. "Before coming here, I was five years in Kenmare. That's down in Kerry," he added.

Gregory looked around the room, which held the musty smell of mildew he associated with older buildings and nursing homes. It was dominated by a large oak desk, which was scrupulously tidy. Along one wall was a bank of locked drawers, which he assumed contained the parish files. On the walls were a series of paintings and framed tapestries, each depicting a religious theme, in case one should forget where they were.

"Aside from being a regular here, how did Claire seem to you?" he asked. "Was she a happy woman, for instance?"

Walsh carried two steaming cups to an overstuffed sofa at one end of the room, and gestured for him to sit.

"I had Connor Byrne in here when it first happened, asking much the same question," he said, settling himself at one end of the faux-leather Chesterfield with an awkward squeak of fabric. "And I told him what I'll tell you now: Claire Kelly seemed to be a very happy woman."

Gregory took a sip of tea, then cupped it in his hands to warm them.

"Father, I'm aware of the rules surrounding confessionals, but since Claire Kelly has passed away, I assume the threat of excommunication no longer applies."

Walsh removed his glasses, rubbed his eyes, then propped them back on his nose.

"It's a common assumption for laypeople to make," he said. "But, on this matter, the Church is clear. The secrecy of a confession is maintained even after the penitent dies. If I were to reveal the contents of Claire's confession, or that of any other person, it would lead to automatic excommunication."

Gregory was silent for a long moment. In his own profession, he abided by strict codes of conduct, so the idea of respecting confidentiality was not alien to him. However, should a patient ever reveal something that conscience dictated was worthy of reporting to the police, he would have no hesitation in doing so in order to prevent a greater evil—confidentiality be damned.

But then, he did not believe in eternal damnation, like the man seated before him.

"Would those rules still apply, even if a man—or woman, say—came to you to confess a murder?"

"Yes, even in those circumstances."

Gregory bore down against a rising tide of frustration.

"What if I were to put it another way, Father. Let's say, in a hypothetical scenario, you were concerned about one of your flock and believed them to be in danger. Would you report your concerns to the police?"

"To do so would invite questions about how I came to be concerned," the priest replied, with a small smile. "I realise this can be hard to accept, but no confessor can be asked to dispense with the need for secrecy, even if he might wish to reveal the contents of a confession to prevent an imminent threat."

Gregory raised his mug in a parody of 'cheers'.

"That's quite a powerful position to be in, Father. I wonder if Liam Kelly would take the same view."

Walsh didn't flinch.

"God willed that man should be left in the hands of his own counsel," he replied, softly.

"Yeah," Gregory muttered, setting the mug down. "Unfortunately, the rest of us have to deal with the consequences. Thanks for the tea, Father."

"Alex?"

He paused.

"My door is always open to those in need. Remember that, my son."

CHAPTER 10

"This is the murder wall."

It was an evocative name, Gregory thought, as he came to stand in front of the long notice board dedicated to Claire Kelly inside the single conference room at the Ballyfinny Garda Station. Unlike the usual boxy, sixties-style architecture he had come to expect of police and government buildings the world over, the town's Garda were housed in a charming, stone-built feat of Victorian architecture that brought to mind visions of *Dixon of Dock Green,* or something equally nostalgic.

The reality was very different. Where Sergeant Connor Byrne might once have relied upon common sense and compassion to police the community he served, that community had begun to lose faith that Claire Kelly's murderer would ever be brought to justice and so demanded the kind of investigative policing found more frequently in cities with high murder rates, and ambitious local politicians. The town called for action and more Garda officers on the streets—as if their presence alone would deter the kind of abnormal mind that had been driven to take a life.

Nonetheless, the mayor had answered the hue and cry, applying pressure so that guards were transferred from neighbouring counties, while her eldest son accepted a temporary transfer from divisional headquarters to preside over the investigation—as well as his brother, whose authority was subordinated by the presence of the inspector who shared his name.

Now, amid the thrum of photocopiers and the plaintive ring of a telephone at the front desk, both men joined Gregory in the Major Incident Room, where they scanned the wall.

"Have there been any developments?" he asked.

"None," Niall said. "We re-interviewed all the neighbours on the street, Claire's family, her friends and work colleagues. Nobody remembers seeing anything unusual around the time she died."

"And their movements are all accounted for?"

"Every last one of them."

Gregory took a step closer to the wall, where a large, blown-up image of a blonde woman was positioned front and centre. In life, Claire Kelly had been an attractive woman of twenty-nine; a school teacher with a loving family and the type of girl-next-door looks other women envied and men desired. It was a dangerous bracket; a kind of median zone where she appeared neither off-putting nor inaccessible to a certain type of predator.

In other words, an ideal target.

"We've got a man watching her grave, but there were no reports of suspicious activity during the funeral," Connor put in.

"It doesn't mean he wasn't there," Gregory said, moving slowly along the wall as he studied each image in turn.

A number of smaller photographs had been tacked to the wall depicting the crime scene and important people in Claire's life, spreading out from her central image in a spider diagram of red string and drawing pins. All of the information was held on a digital case file and there were computer programs that served the same purpose, but he happened to agree there was no substitute for the immediate impact of a physical wall.

"What's your working theory?" he asked. "You've already told me you believe it was someone from outside the area."

Niall folded his arms, tucking his hands into his armpits in what Gregory recognised as a fighting stance.

"Sex crime," he said, bluntly. "It's true, we've found no semen at the scene, or on Claire, but who's to say the bastard wasn't impotent? You hear about that sort—the type who can't get it up and then take it out on women."

Connor nodded his agreement.

"We heard all you said about it being someone from the town," he added. "But, God's truth, there isn't anybody here who fits the bill."

Gregory leaned against one of the freestanding desks and braced his hands either side, choosing his words with care.

"I've seen cases where killers or rapists attack without being able to enact the sexual element to their fantasy," he said. "But I read the autopsy report you gave me, and it was categorical. There was no evidence of sexual assault. In cases such as the one you've described, the assailant usually at least *attempts* to follow through."

He looked up at the pictures of Claire, then back at the other two men in the room.

"The autopsy report also said the initial, immobilising blow struck the back of her head. You've told me the weapon was most likely a heavy ornament from the table in her hallway. That tells us something very important."

"He was quick," Connor remarked. "And an opportunist."

"She turned her back on him," Niall muttered, and sat down to rest his forearms on his knees in a gesture of defeat. "Claire turned away from him."

Gregory nodded.

"Claire Kelly either knew her killer or trusted them enough, in a very short space of time, to allow them entry to her home. She was pregnant, too, which usually means higher levels of self-preservation."

"Could have been a delivery man," Connor argued. "Or some salesperson."

"It could," Gregory nodded. "Except nobody remembers seeing a van or an unusual car parked outside. They would have had to bring their own transportation to pull this off, unless they knew the area or lived nearby."

He pushed away from the table and walked to the board again, this time looking into the smiling, slightly cocksure eyes of the man Liam Kelly had been a month before his world had changed irrevocably.

"I know you don't want to believe it, but I think you have to accept it," he said. "The likelihood is, somebody watched her come and go, took the time to learn her routines. They couldn't have made several trips to the area without being seen, unless they're already part of the landscape."

Connor kicked the edge of the wall, and began pacing the floor like a caged animal.

"Bastard's sitting right under our noses," he snarled.

"Aye," Niall agreed, in a tired voice. "He's been sitting here all along."

CHAPTER 11

The three men spent another hour going over the facts, then began to dissect the minutiae of Claire Kelly's life. She was the second daughter of a respectable, working-class family, who'd attended the local school before university in neighbouring Galway, and had a loyal circle of friends from both counties to show for it. Leafing through the statements given by them and her work colleagues, many of whom she counted as friends, Gregory began to form a picture of a wholesome, clean-living woman who had been universally liked. She had no criminal record; not even a token point on her driving licence for speeding.

It made him suspicious.

"What aren't you telling me?" he asked. "What's missing from the file?"

Connor opened his mouth to speak but one look from his brother silenced him.

"What makes you think anything's missing?" Niall asked.

Gregory raised the sheaf of paper he held in his hand, then dropped it on the table.

"Nobody's this squeaky-clean," he said.

The other two shifted uncomfortably in their seats.

"It came out when we were taking a statement from a bloke called Tom Reilly. He's the headmaster at the school where Claire worked," Niall said, heavily. "The man's married with two kids and his wife was one of Claire's friends. He claims they had an affair a couple of years ago, and begged us not to tell anyone. Said he needed to get it off his chest, in case we found anything at her house and tried to pin him with her murder."

Gregory frowned.

"It doesn't seem consistent with her personality," he murmured, but then his face cleared as he remembered something from her medical records. "When was this alleged affair?"

"Tom says it happened about six months after Emily was born," Connor replied. "Going on two years ago. Why?"

"According to her GP notes, Claire was suffering from moderately-severe postpartum depression," Gregory replied. "It can lead to rash decision-making and actions that are generally out of character, owing to fluctuating hormone levels. The timing fits, but I don't understand why this information would be withheld from the file."

"Look, you don't know how things work around here—" Niall shoved away from the desk where he'd been sitting and walked across to stand in front of Gregory's chair, just a fraction too close for comfort.

"I think I'm beginning to," Alex drawled, and deliberately relaxed his body.

He'd completed all kinds of self-defence training, which was mandatory for a man in his position at the hospital, but violence was seldom his first port of call. At Southmoor, there had been many times when he'd diffused a volatile situation with a few, well-timed words and nothing more.

"Does your mother know that you doctor the police files?" he asked the inspector. "As mayor, she has a right to expect the Garda will perform their duties to a professional standard. A man in your position should be well aware of that."

Niall's head snapped back as if he'd been struck, so Connor stepped into the breach.

"Our mother—*the mayor*—would understand that it serves no purpose to make that kind of thing public knowledge. It risks breaking up Tom Reilly's marriage, and smashing to pieces the memory Liam Kelly has of his wife. All because they had some fling, over two years ago," he argued.

"Shall we ask her?" Gregory wondered aloud.

There was a short, tense silence, then Niall stepped away.

"You've made your point."

Gregory stood up and met him eye to eye.

"I'm here to help, but I can't do that if there isn't full disclosure. If we're looking at somebody local, that means everybody's in the frame—including Tom Reilly. I need your assurance that the file will be updated, and that you won't cut me out again."

"He's right," Connor muttered. "Before, when we thought we were looking for an outsider, that was one thing, but, now…"

"Reilly doesn't have an alibi," his brother said flatly. "I know."

Gregory looked between them.

"What about his wife?"

Both men looked up in surprise, then Connor reached for the file and thumbed through a thick pile of statements until he found the one he was looking for.

"Kate Reilly says that, while Tom was out jogging, she was at home all morning."

"With the kids?" Niall asked, but Connor shook his head.

"They were at their grandparents' house."

"In other words, neither of their movements are accounted for," Gregory said. "We need to narrow the search pool, starting with those who had the means and opportunity to be at Claire Kelly's home between the hours of eight-thirty and ten-thirty in the morning, every Saturday."

"Every Saturday?" Connor queried. "Just on the day she died, surely?"

"If we assume her killer kept her under surveillance, they needed to observe the family routine every Saturday morning. Start with the Reillys."

"I can't see either of them—"

"Forget the people you think you know," Gregory cut across another protestation from Connor. "You don't know this man or woman as you think you do. You only know the part they allow you to see. Unless they make some mistake, or otherwise show themselves, we'll need to flush them out, somehow. Start with some old-fashioned policing, then we'll look at the psychology of those we have left."

Connor swallowed.

"If I really try to imagine it, I could see a man doing that to Claire. But a woman?"

Gregory almost smiled. Apparently, it was a case of 'like mother, like son', when it came to stereotyping killer profiles.

"Think of the staging," he said. "Women are, statistically, more likely to commit a 'clean' murder. They don't strike out in the heat of the moment. In Claire's case, her killer had a very specific idea of how they wanted her to die. A woman could easily have done it; more easily, if she was already Claire's friend."

"You're thinking, maybe, Kate Reilly found out about the affair?" Niall asked.

"I'm opening your mind to the possibilities," Gregory replied.

He moved across to look at a large, aerial photograph of Ballyfinny that covered another wall of the Incident Room. The Kelly home was already marked with a red drawing pin, and he studied the roads and pathways around it.

"I need to visit the house," he said quietly. "I need to see what they saw."

Niall watched Gregory from across the room and wondered how he'd ever missed what was blindingly obvious to anybody who bothered to look.

"You care about him," he realised. "The one we're looking for."

Gregory gave an almost imperceptible nod, while he continued to study the map.

"Almost as much as I care about Claire, and all the other people who might be hurt if we don't bring him in."

"The Kelly house is still closed up," Connor said. "Liam and Emily are staying with his parents. Poor bloke says he can't face going back, and he told me this morning he's planning to sell up. We can go and take a look at the house anytime."

"What do you expect to find?" Niall asked.

"Shadows," Gregory replied, and left it at that.

CHAPTER 12

The Kelly house was located on the southern edge of the town, halfway back to the Ballyfinny Castle Hotel. It was the last plot along a winding country lane that traced the edge of the lough and served a row of five or six large, modern one-storey houses built on high ground, affording panoramic views of the water and hills in the distance. On the other side of the road, the land undulated down to the shore and was heavily wooded, but for a small footpath which led down to a small landing jetty where local residents could moor their boats.

"Nice area," Connor said, as he brought his police vehicle to a stop at the side of the road. Niall Byrne had remained at the Garda station to deal with a mountain of other tasks, which continued to pile in from the wider division, entrusting his younger brother to introduce their visitor to the crime scene.

Gregory made a non-committal sound as he stepped out of the passenger side and into the late afternoon air, which was damp with the promise of rain and heavy with the scent of pine that seemed to cloak that corner of the county.

"In for a storm, I reckon," Connor remarked, walking around the bonnet to join him on the narrow pavement.

Gregory was only half listening while his eyes scanned the immediate vicinity. Connor Byrne was right; the Kelly family lived in a beautiful spot, which must have set them back a pretty penny, given the price of land thereabouts—but it was isolated. There may have been four other houses on the street, but the closest was out of sight, beyond the bend in the road where the land curved in line with the lough. He imagined, when Claire and Liam Kelly had first come to look at their new plot, they'd have seen only an ideal home: near enough to town but detached and not overlooked by any neighbours. For those who preferred privacy and the Great Outdoors, it was the perfect location.

They could never have imagined that such an idyll could prove to be their worst nightmare but, as he stood beneath the gathering storm, Gregory could see it all so clearly. He saw the long, country lane without the twitch of neighbouring curtains; the dense wood, which provided cover to anybody seeking to hide within its fold; and, most of all, he saw the chocolate-box house with its wainscoted walls painted in pristine white—a perfect picture just begging to be despoiled. He saw the wide windows with curtains that were rarely drawn, and the side gate to the back garden that, even now, swung on its hinges and whose lock was probably stiff and rusted from lack of use.

A playground, for a certain kind of killer.

Gregory realised Connor had asked him something, and was waiting for a response.

"Sorry," he said. "I was miles away."

"Yeah, it gets that way," Connor said, with a small shrug. "Cases like these work their way under your skin, so it's hard to think about much else. Shall we go inside?"

Gregory followed him up a short, paved driveway to the front door, which still held the remnants of police tape that was starting to come loose.

"No signs of forced entry," Connor said, though both men knew it already. "None at the back of the house, either."

He fiddled with a large ring of keys, trying several until he found the right one.

"What're the other ones for?" Gregory asked.

Connor looked down at the keys and jiggled them in the palm of his hand.

"Another quirk of a small town," he explained, with a smile. "Most people drop into the station with a spare key, in case they go on holiday and their house alarm starts going off, or they lock themselves out, or some such."

"People are trusting, in these parts."

"Aye, they are," Connor said, and pushed open the door.

———

Inside, their nostrils were assailed by the lingering scent of iodine.

"Haven't had the cleaners in here, yet," Connor explained, and brushed an idle finger against a thin layer of black fingerprinting powder.

"It's better that way," Gregory said, and closed his eyes briefly to imagine Claire Kelly making her way down the hallway towards the front door, not stopping to check the peephole before she threw it open to the person who planned to take it all from her.

"Is that where the ornament used to be?" he asked, nodding towards a narrow console table pushed against the wall.

Connor nodded.

"It's in the Evidence Store," he explained. "Lab sent it back to us a week or so ago."

The table was three or four paces from the front door, Gregory noted—close enough for any opportunist to reach past Claire in the doorway to grab it.

"They had to gain entry first, before they picked up the ornament," he murmured.

Connor folded his arms.

"Forensics team found a couple of drops of blood on the carpet—there—and another partial droplet on the wall," he said. "There'd been a decent attempt to clean it up."

"I wonder why they bothered, if they planned to leave Claire for her family to find," Gregory mused. "There was no need to do an extensive clean-up, since they had no intention of trying to conceal her murder."

Connor rubbed the edge of his thumb against the side of his nose while he mulled it over, then gave another one of his light shrugs.

"Maybe he didn't want to mess her house up," he offered.

Gregory looked at him for a long moment.

"Maybe you're right," he said, then gestured along the hallway. "He took her to the bathroom, next?"

"Far as we can tell," Connor agreed. "It's along this way."

Gregory followed the sergeant along the wide hallway and, despite all the upheaval, he could see how it might have been on the day Claire Kelly died. The walls were painted in the palest sage green, and photographs of her family lined the walls in classy, black-and-white prints, framed in white wood. As they passed the kitchen, he saw acres of pristine granite countertops and a fridge covered in Emily's drawings. Neat as a pin, without being a show home.

"Bathroom's in here," Connor said, and stood aside to allow Gregory to precede him.

And, when he took his first step across the threshold, he felt a wave of sadness; so strong, he almost braced a hand against the wall. The rational part of himself recognised the emotion for what it was: a projection of what he already knew had happened inside the bathroom, with its unassuming porcelain-tiled floor and watercolour seascape on the wall. Were it not for the remaining fingerprint dust clinging to the sink, and the gaping holes where the taps ought to have been, he might never have known a woman had died here—there was no blood, no gore.

Only emptiness.

"Forensics took the taps and pipework away," Connor said, from somewhere over his right shoulder.

"The pathologist report said the knife blow went straight into her aorta," Gregory said. "With that kind of injury, it would have taken less than five minutes for her to bleed out, and her clothes would have been covered."

He turned back to the sergeant.

"When Emily and Liam found her, and in the crime scene images, Claire Kelly's clothes have no bloodstains, which means he must've changed her clothing after hosing her down in here. What happened to the blood-stained clothes?"

"We never found them," Connor said. "They're missing, along with the knife."

When Gregory said nothing, he stepped inside the room and took another cursory glance around.

"D'you reckon the killer took the clothes as a kind of trophy? Sometimes, they take little bits and bobs with them."

"It would hardly be little bits and bobs, in this case," Gregory pointed out. "He wouldn't want to be seen lugging a bag full of bloodied clothes around the place, if he was making off on foot. Maybe he had to take the clothing because he was afraid some of his DNA had rubbed off."

Connor's lips thinned.

"Aye, that could be it."

Gregory took one final look around the room, then stepped back into the hallway, a light sweat breaking out on the back of his neck along with a sense of foreboding. Small spaces could do that.

Small spaces, and dark places.

As he made his way towards the end of the long, central corridor which ran the breadth of the house, Gregory's sense of foreboding grew stronger. Tiny hairs prickled on the back of his neck, as though somebody was right beside him.

But, when he spun around, he found Connor Byrne still standing at the other end of the hallway speaking on his smartphone, having taken a call from the station.

Alone with his thoughts, Gregory turned back to the door marked, 'EMILY'S ROOM' in wooden lettering shaped like animals, and pushed it open.

The little girl's bedroom had been decorated in shades of pink and cream, fit for a princess. A tiny, chiffon canopy had been arranged above the bed, which was the only part that remained untouched by the forensics team, who had seized the mattress, coverings and toys for examination. All the same, he had seen pictures of how it had been and, if he closed his eyes, he could still visualise the scene that had greeted Emily Kelly when she'd come home from swimming practice.

He stood in the centre of the room for long, long minutes, and did not hear Connor's quiet tread along the corridor outside until the man was almost within touching distance.

"Doc?"

Gregory's eyes flew open, and he raised his arms in a reflex action, keeping his guard high.

"Whoa, there! Easy, feller! Sorry, I didn't mean to give you a start," Connor said, holding his hands out.

Gregory lowered his hands slowly, keeping his eyes trained on the other man.

"Guess you didn't hear me," Connor said, and gave a nervous laugh. For a mild-mannered criminal profiler, Alex Gregory bore the look of a man ready to kill, or be killed. "I s'pose working in a max-security hospital makes you kind of jumpy."

Gregory worked up some semblance of a smile.

"You could say that."

Connor made a cursory inspection of the room, then stuck his hands in the back pockets of his jeans.

"One of the theories we had is that whoever killed Claire was really looking for her daughter, and that's why they set her up in here," he said.

Gregory was unconvinced.

"If Claire was collateral damage, or second choice, they wouldn't have taken such time and trouble with her," he murmured, and turned slowly to look at the placement of items in the room. "Did you do an inventory of everything in here?"

Connor lifted a shoulder.

"We made a list of everything we took away for testing, if that's what you mean. Liam Kelly signed it."

Gregory could have laughed at that. A grieving widower would sign anything, if only it would bring his wife back.

"I mean everything in the room, not just the things taken away by the forensics team," he said. "It's possible Claire's killer might have taken that trophy you were talking about."

Connor came to attention.

"I can get a team in here today," he said. "We'll run it past Liam sometime tomorrow or next week, give him a chance to get over the shock of the funeral."

Gregory knew that was the right and proper thing to do, but the hunter in him wanted action there and then.

"Let me know if he says anything's missing," was all he said.

"If they weren't after the kid, why did they set Claire up in here?" Connor asked.

Gregory met his eyes across the room, then raised a hand to point at a large, clear-glass window looking out over the back garden. It dominated one wall of the bedroom and was framed in pale pink curtains with a pattern of white stars.

"They watched her through this window, lying on the bed here, reading Claire a bedtime story," he said, in a voice so low Connor strained to hear him. "Sitting in a perfect home, in a perfect world, at least from the outside. Maybe they wanted a slice of the fairy tale."

Connor moved to the window, where he looked out across the garden, which was becoming overgrown.

"On the map, there's a footpath which runs behind the garden fence," Gregory said. "Where does it lead?"

Connor didn't bother to turn around.

"If you follow the path west, it takes you back into the centre of town," he said. "If you go east, it leads you through the trees to the hotel."

"Have you searched the footpath?"

"We've gone over the whole area," Connor told him. "We found nothing."

"Try again," Gregory said. "Look for plastic residue, or charred earth. He wouldn't want to carry her clothing back into town, so there's a chance he burned it."

Connor nodded, and continued to look out across the garden.

"Can you help somebody like that? What if they're too far gone?"

"Nobody is beyond redemption," Gregory said quietly. "It can take years of intensive therapy, but people can change."

He had to believe it, or go mad himself.

CHAPTER 13

Later, when the rain had begun to patter a melody against the windowpanes of her little cottage, Aideen McArdle set a steaming bowl of potatoes on the dining room table and settled down to eat with her family.

"Colm, you go easy on that butter," she said, watching her husband scoop a dollop onto his plate. "You know what the doctor said about your cholesterol."

He made a raspberry sound.

"I'm as fit as a fiddle," he said. "My old Da ate a full Irish breakfast every morning and he lived to be ninety-one."

Aideen pursed her lips.

"That's as maybe," she said, obliquely. "But the doctor—"

"Now, don't fret yourself," he said, and deliberately scraped the butter to one side of his plate. "I'll be here to pester you for many more years to come, the good Lord willing."

Aideen reached across the table to grasp her husband's hand. She looked down at their crinkled skin, marred by age spots and hard work, and gave his fingers a squeeze.

"There, now," she said, briskly. "Who's for some more of this beef?"

Her children and grandchildren crowded around the table beside her, still dressed in black from the funeral earlier that day. As she watched her daughter-in-law spoon vegetables onto a plate for the youngest member of the McArdle family, she thought of Claire Kelly and those she had left behind. It was a terrible thing for a child to lose its mother, and she could only be grateful that her own kin hadn't been touched by such tragedy.

When their plates were piled high, they joined hands and said a prayer for the departed. They were illuminated by a lampshade overhead, framing their bent heads in a backdrop of warm yellow light inside the window, which stood out like a beacon through the falling rain.

To the one who watched, they seemed unreal; a perfect microcosm of what 'family life' should be. Though there was no sound, they could imagine the laughter, and, with a little effort, they could lip-read what Aideen was saying to the children who came and pressed their sticky faces to her chest.

"Run along and play," she told the youngest. *"Wash your hands before you go near my sofa!"*

Her warmth spread across the cold evening air and, to their addled brain, her smile might have been meant for them, and them alone.

The showers grew heavier as the afternoon became early evening. Gregory made a dash through the rain, dodging puddles as he followed the directions he'd been given to Maggie's house, where he was invited for dinner. Mayor Byrne's home turned out to be more than 'a quick stretch of the legs' from the centre of town, and he was beginning to regret not taking up the offer of a lift as he rounded a corner and was faced with another steep, cobbled incline. There were no road signs and, with the rain falling in every direction, he could barely make out any light at its summit. He raised a hand to shield his eyes, peered through the gloom and then, with a fatalistic shrug, dug in his heels and jogged lightly up the hill, clutching a bottle of wine he'd bought from a little shop on the way.

To his relief, Maggie's house awaited him at the top. Like most things in Ballyfinny, it was a quaint, modest affair; white-painted with a dark green front door. When the rain was not falling in sheets, he imagined it would enjoy breathtaking views but, for the present, he was more concerned with the shelter it afforded indoors.

Four cars were parked on the road outside; two of which he recognised as belonging to Niall and Connor Byrne, and one he assumed belonged to Maggie—but he wondered about the fourth. None of the Byrne family had mentioned a family patriarch, and the mayor wore no wedding ring, so he'd assumed she was a divorcee or had chosen not to marry Connor and Niall's father, good manners having prevented him from enquiring further.

Perhaps there was a Mr Byrne Senior, after all.

Gregory hurried up a short pathway towards a covered porch with a hanging lantern, which was swinging wildly as the wind picked up. He ducked underneath and shook out the waterproof raincoat he'd borrowed from the hotel. Water ran in rivulets across his face and he pushed dark, wet hair back from his forehead, no longer the smartly-dressed, city psychologist but a man caught in the rain, like any other.

He raised a hand to rap his knuckles on the door, which had neither a knocker nor a bell, a fact he found entirely in keeping with the owner's personality. Maggie Byrne was not the sort of woman to invite idle knocking at her door, nor to display gaudy brass knockers in the shape of prancing animals.

Presently, he heard the sound of footsteps approaching and squared his shoulders, preparing to greet the lady herself.

But, when the door opened, another woman stood on the threshold; one with long, slender limbs and hair the colour of spun gold.

"Emma?"

The woman he'd met briefly that morning smiled, though it didn't quite reach her eyes.

"Hello, again."

They were cocooned for a moment in time while they measured one another. Then, she gestured for him to step inside.

"You'd better come in," she said. "Dinner's nearly ready."

Gregory shrugged out of his coat and hung it from one of the pegs inside the porch, then joined her in the hallway. Emma shut the door to the wind and then seemed to hesitate, but any conversation was forestalled by the arrival of the lady of the house.

"There you are," Maggie said, as her head appeared around the kitchen doorway. "Thought we'd have to send out a search party. Did you get lost?"

"A couple of times," he admitted. "Ever think of putting up some street signs around here?"

The mayor let out a short, booming laugh that ricocheted around the walls.

"Why bother? It's more fun watching outsiders wander around in the rain. Come on in, and dry yourself," she said.

Gregory followed Emma down the hallway to a cosy kitchen that gleamed with polished copper pans which hung from a rack in the centre of the room, where a chunky wooden table had been set for six.

"It's not much, but it's mine," Maggie smiled, and wiped her hands on a striped tea towel. "I see you've already met my daughter-in-law."

Not a flicker of emotion passed over Gregory's face, which remained entirely neutral as she imparted the information.

"We met very briefly this morning," he said, and turned to look at the woman standing a careful distance away from him. "Which brother are you married to?"

"I married Niall seven years ago," Emma said, quietly.

An awkward silence fell, then Maggie cleared her throat.

"The boys are in the living room," she said. "Would you ask them to come through, love?"

Emma's eyes passed over him as she left, and his skin prickled as though it had been burned.

"They've been having a few troubles," Maggie explained, once they were alone. "They're trying to work through them, for Declan's sake. That's my grandson."

"I'm sorry."

Maggie nodded, assuming that he was sorry for their troubles, and not because they were making an effort to resolve them.

He was a healer first and always, Gregory thought, with some resentment. *Not a red-blooded man like any other.*

"Can I help with anything?" he asked, to distract himself.

But Maggie shooed him away, so he uncorked the bottle of wine he'd brought and set it on the table to breathe.

Then, picked it up again and poured them both a glass.

"Well, if it isn't the shaman, himself," Niall declared, as he entered the kitchen.

Gregory shook the man's hand, and a quick assessment told him the inspector had already made a head start on the alcohol.

"You found us, then," Connor said, taking a seat beside him at the table.

"I might take you up on that lift, next time," Gregory joked.

"Declan's happy watching cartoons on TV," Emma said, taking a seat beside her husband.

"He should learn to sit and have dinner with us," Niall replied, and started to get up again to go in search of his son.

"He's happy," she muttered, her eyes begging him not to make an issue of it. "Why not leave him to it? He'll be bored listening to adult conversation, and I don't want him to overhear anything about Claire."

"I'll take him a supper plate later," Maggie said, and placed a firm hand on her son's shoulder before he could argue. "Declan will soon tell us, if he's hungry before then."

The matter decided, she took her seat at the head of the table.

"Well, don't let it go cold," she declared.

They helped themselves to bowls of meatballs marinara before Maggie spoke again.

"I had Liam Kelly at my door again, today," she said, without rancour. "He wants to meet you, Alex."

"Is that a good idea?" Connor wondered. "Liam's hurting. He doesn't know what he wants, or needs."

Gregory swallowed, then set his fork down.

"Liam needs compassion," he said softly, and Emma looked up to meet his eyes across the table.

He was the first to look away.

"I'm not here in a clinical capacity, but I'm here to profile his wife's killer," he continued. "The man needs some reassurance that I'm here to help bring justice for Claire, not somebody who's out to make a name for himself."

Niall sloshed more wine into his glass, and took a long drink, swilling the liquid around his mouth before swallowing.

"Maybe you are, maybe you aren't," he muttered, not quite under his breath. "It's why you get into the business, isn't it? To get inside people's heads and feel superior, while people tell you how bloody good you are?"

Gregory was torn between anger and pity, but one look at Maggie's face decided it. There was history here, he realised, something he knew nothing about.

Pity won.

"Maybe some people go into psychology to understand themselves better," he replied, and took his time twirling a fork around a long string of spaghetti. "Getting inside people's heads, as you put it, is really a way of understanding their own."

He felt Emma's eyes on him again, but did not meet them this time.

"As for making a name for myself, I've already made one," he continued. "I don't need another. I have my own work waiting for me in London and the patients there aren't all household names. They're ordinary people the world will never know. For various reasons, they took the wrong path and need guidance to get back onto the right one. Some make it, others don't."

He spoke directly to Niall.

"I'm not superhuman; none of us are. Psychologists and psychiatrists, and everybody else working in the field, are mortals and that means we make mistakes, sometimes. I'm sorry if somebody made a mistake in the past, and it cost you, Niall. But, right now, I want the same thing you do. I want to help Liam Kelly sleep soundly at night, knowing the person who killed his wife won't be doing the same thing to anybody else."

"Oh yeah?" Niall said. "What if we don't find him? What if he's too good for us, and we never find him? What do we tell Liam Kelly, then?"

"You *will* find him," Gregory said quietly.

"How do you know?" Connor toyed with a meatball on his plate. "He's ahead of us, so far."

"Whoever makes the first move will always be one step ahead," Maggie remarked. "It's a game of catch-up, to begin with."

Gregory nodded slowly.

"Exactly. There's always a pattern. It's just a matter of finding it and understanding the killer's motivation."

"Who cares what his motivation is?" Niall burst out. "Who bloody cares what this maniac thinks?"

"It helps us to understand why he does what he does," Gregory replied. "By looking at why he chose Claire, we can understand what makes him tick. I'm not asking you to empathise with his reasons, I'm asking you to consider what they were."

"She was gentle," Emma said, looking around the table. "Claire tried to be firm with the kids at school, but they had her wrapped around their little fingers, most of the time. God rest her."

It fitted Gregory's image of Claire Kelly as an accessible target.

"How she was likely to react to danger would have been a major contributing factor, when her killer made his choice.

When they sense danger, some women will freeze, like a deer in the headlights," he said, keeping his voice down in case Declan should overhear. "Others will fight, tooth and nail."

"And some go looking for danger," Emma finished for him.

This time, he met her gaze.

"Yes," he said softly. "Or it finds them."

***

That night, Alex dreamed of a woman with long, red hair.

She walked ahead and just out of reach, leading him along a pathway through the woods. Rain beat down upon them both, plastering the shirt to his back as he hurried to keep her in sight. He reached out to touch her, but she spun away, laughing, her skin pale and sleek as she blinked water from her eyes.

He smiled too, and felt weightless with a lightness of being he hadn't experienced in a very long time.

Perhaps never.

She started to run, faster and faster as she led him further along the path. He kept pace with her, legs burning as the surrounding woodland became a blur, feet skidding against the sodden earth as he tried not to fall.

He never wanted to fall.

Eventually, her footsteps slowed and then stopped beside a long wooden fence bordering one side of the path. He came to stand beside her and reached out his hand again, but his fingers found nothing but air.

He spun around, searching for her.

"Emma? Where are you? Where did you go?"

But she was nowhere to be found, and he started to panic.

"Emma! Come back! It's not safe!"

His eye fell on a small chink in the fence, where one of the wooden slats had come loose. A single strand of long, red hair was caught on the edge, and he crouched down to tug it away. When he did, the slat swung to one side, revealing a narrow gap. Through it, he saw a garden with a well-tended lawn and a long, white-painted wooden house with large windows. In one of them, a pale pink lampshade burned brightly while a red-haired woman and her son read a storybook on a small child's bed.

Emma.

He tried to rush forward, but his clothes caught on the fence and surrounding branches, which nipped at his skin.

"Emma! Don't stay there! It's not safe!"

He twisted and turned to free himself, but the grip seemed to tighten and, when he looked again, he realised it was not branches that held him back.

It was two people.

"I'll look after the little boy," Cathy Jones whispered, while her purple-painted hands gripped his right arm.

"It's God's will," Father Walsh said, gripping the left.

Gregory fought against them, thrashing wildly until he broke free of the nightmare and returned to reality, but not before he heard the soft sound of a baby's cry.

CHAPTER 14

Sunday

After a restless night, Gregory spent much of the early hours compiling a long list of residents who, by their own admission, had the logistical means and opportunity to have killed Claire Kelly. Her assailant was more likely to be male, so he prioritised that gender but did not discount the possibility of there being another motive for her death; particularly, given what he had learned about Claire's former relationship with Tom Reilly, the headmaster at the school where she worked.

Revenge was as good a motive as any, particularly for a woman scorned.

A cold cup of coffee stood on the desk beside him, the milk having formed a floating crust sometime during the past four hours since he'd last touched it, and Gregory took that as a sign it was time to move on. He was due back at Southmoor Hospital by Monday morning, so he'd booked a late flight back to London that evening. In the intervening hours, he hoped to learn as much as he could about Claire's friends and neighbours, especially those whose names were now written inside his notebook. Since it was Sunday, many of those people would be attending Mass, so he decided to overcome his natural aversion to religious ceremonies and join them.

He ran into Seamus Murphy and Padraig as he left the hotel a short while later, and the two men walked companionably beside him along the country lane towards Ballyfinny.

Gregory knew that Padraig lived in a small groundskeeper's cottage down near the waterside, and the manager of the hotel kept an apartment on one of the upper floors of the castle, so he could be on hand to deal with any emergency as it arose. Today, both men were dressed in their 'Sunday Best', consisting of suit, shirt and tie—though they wore sturdy walking shoes for the journey along the woodland lane. The rain had stopped sometime during the night, but the ground remained damp and their feet squelched through layers of fallen leaves and mulch. It was hard to mind, since the storm had cleared the way for blue, cloudless skies, allowing sunlight to filter unhindered through the trees in shards of dappled light. There was a freshness to the air, Alex thought—as though the rain had washed away the sins of yesterday, leaving a fresh canvas upon which they could paint something new.

"Maggie tells me you're giving Niall and Connor plenty of food for thought," Seamus said, after they'd walked for a few minutes in comfortable silence. "Are you getting any closer?"

Gregory was circumspect.

"We're making some progress," he said.

"Can't come soon enough," Seamus replied. "It's hard on the boys."

Gregory glanced across at his profile, then back to the road ahead.

"It's impossible not to be affected during a murder investigation," he agreed.

"Aye, but it'll be a reminder of their Da," Seamus said, and Padraig made a grunting sound of disapproval in the back of his throat, as if to warn against the revelation.

"'Tis over and done wit," he muttered. "And best forgotten."

Seamus ignored him.

"Maggie's husband, my brother-in-law, was murdered back in '83. IRA came into the house and shot him dead, right there in his own home, with Niall playing on the rug at his feet."

Gregory digested the new information, imagining the unspeakable trauma and what it might do to a person.

"What about Connor?" he asked, in a low voice. "Did he see it happen, too?"

Seamus's brow furrowed, then cleared again.

"You mustn't have heard—and Maggie never talks of it. She adopted Connor a few years later…must've been back in '87 or '88, when he was five, or thereabouts."

"Six," Padraig put in. "And nothing more'n a skinny bag of bones, when he arrived on her doorstep."

"I had no idea," Gregory said. "Niall and Connor look so alike."

But, the more he thought about it, the more he realised he'd seen only what the world expected to see of two brothers. In reality, the differences in looks and temperament were stark.

"Maggie was lonely after Aiden went," her brother explained. "She always wanted a houseful of children, and a brother or sister for Niall."

"Found him at the children's home down in Galway," Padraig put in. "Awful place. Government shut it down, a few years back."

Gregory thought of the scandal surrounding the old orphanages run by Catholic nuns who had, it seemed, forgotten the basic tenets of their faith.

"Connor knew Father Walsh from the old days at the orphanage," Seamus continued, as the abbey spire came into view, peeping over the surrounding rooftops.

"They must be around the same age—surely, he couldn't have known Father Walsh?"

"I don't mean he knew him as a priest," Seamus said. "I mean they were boys together, at St. Hilda's Orphanage. Must've been a surprise to find an old friend living in the same town."

Gregory nodded, and began to wonder about the coincidence.

Was there any such thing?

Perhaps; but one thing he was sure about—early life trauma could impair the development of important emotions, such as compassion and empathy, both of which were crucial to prevent a person enacting violent thoughts and fantasies, including murder. Without human compassion, the victim was just a body—a means to an end—and so much easier to kill.

The very definition of what it meant to be a psychopath.

"Like I say, the sooner all this is tied up, the better," Seamus said. "Those boys have been through enough."

Gregory nodded, his eyes on the priest who stood at the entrance to the abbey, greeting his congregation as they made their way into Mass. He watched Sean Walsh shaking hands and smiling, every action unthreatening and prosaic, and wondered what memories lay behind the man's myopic brown eyes.

***

The church was not heaving with the same crowd that had gathered the day before, its number having reverted to usual proportions as the practising Catholics of the town piled inside to worship. Gregory, Padraig and Seamus joined the queue to enter, waiting their turn to be welcomed by the priest.

"Seamus, it's good to see you again," Walsh said, when the man stepped forward. "We missed you, last week."

"Yes, I'm sorry, Father. We had a few troubles at the hotel."

"I understand, I understand. And Padraig, how's that leg holding up?"

The man tapped a hand to his hip, which Gregory assumed to have been ailing him.

"It's better, Father. Much better, thank you."

"Well, well. That's good. And, I see you've brought Doctor Gregory with you. Welcome back, Alex."

"Thank you, Father," he replied, with stiff politeness.

"Will you take Communion with us, today?"

Gregory had a sudden, flashing memory of a hard circle being pressed onto his tongue as a small boy, and barely repressed a shudder.

"Not today, Father, but thank you."

Walsh nodded and then, to Gregory's surprise, closed his eyes and made the sign of the cross while he performed a very quick blessing.

"I—thank you," he managed, and walked quickly inside the wide oak doors.

In contrast with the previous day, Gregory found the atmosphere positively convivial within the abbey walls. Immediately inside the doorway, new arrivals dipped their fingers into a font of holy water and crossed themselves before taking a seat, but he couldn't bring himself to do the same. Instead, he moved to the wall, not far from where he'd stood the day before, and leaned back against the cold stone to observe.

He watched a smartly-dressed woman somewhere in her late seventies arrive on the arm of a man who must have been her husband, both moving slowly but sure-footedly with a couple of grandchildren in tow.

"Colm? Tell Mary-Louise to stop splashing in the holy water!"

Gregory smiled at the tableau, and watched the girl's grandfather amble across to pluck the small child up and into his arms.

"C'mon, munchkin. Time for Sunday School," he said.

Gregory watched them move away, a small smile playing on his lips. There was still good in the world, he thought, and it was worth protecting.

A moment later, Emma entered the church holding Declan's small hand, while Niall followed a couple of paces behind them looking slightly the worse for wear. It had been an uneasy dinner the night before, and an uncomfortable insight into their domestic circumstances. The inspector had polished off almost two bottles of wine to himself before the meal was over, not counting what he put away before and after, which went some way to explaining why his wife was so very unhappy.

His eyes strayed to where Emma was talking with another woman from the town, and he savoured the sight of her before he was discovered.

It came sooner than he would have liked.

"Morning, Alex," Maggie said, spotting him as soon as she entered. "Didn't expect to see you here."

"I was raised Catholic," he said, but did not elaborate.

"Are you coming to sit down?" she asked, and he sensed a kind of desperation to her voice.

He shook his head. It wouldn't help to torment himself, or to imagine taking up what had been offered—in everything but words.

Distance was required.

"I plan to make a quick getaway," he joked. "Besides, there's a better view from here."

Maggie shuffled her feet, which were clad in navy woollen tights tucked inside a pair of chunky walking boots he suspected only she could wear with such aplomb.

"I'll drive you to the airport, later," she said. "I'd like the chance to talk to you privately."

When she moved off to join her family, he wondered what new revelations would be in store.

The profiler was there.

They could *feel* his eyes sweeping around the church, tracing the rows of heads, wondering which of them was the wolf amongst the flock of sheep.

At first, they'd been afraid.

They'd imagined the man would be able to see through skulls, or peel away their skin to uncover their deepest, most shameful heart.

But he could do neither.

He was but a man.

"Therefore, just as through one man sin entered the world, and death through sin, and so death spread to all men, because all sinned…"

Yes, one man had sinned, and death now spread like a virus.

It would not stop.

It could not.

CHAPTER 15

"That's Tom Reilly, over there."

Gregory met the Garda detectives outside the church, where Sergeant Connor Byrne pointed out the headmaster of the local school as he left Sunday Mass with his wife and children. He was a good-looking man, who glanced briefly towards them, before ushering his family away.

"He's nervous," Niall said, and began to walk slowly in the other direction towards the Garda station. "We haven't come across anybody who can corroborate his story about being out jogging on the Saturday Claire died, so maybe he's got something to be nervous about."

But Gregory was more interested in Reilly's wife, a petite blonde who seemed not to have noticed the line of Garda men eyeing her husband with such interest.

Her physicality put a question mark over her ability to have handled a body, but working at Southmoor had taught him that physical appearance alone was not determinative of anything.

"We never found any of Reilly's DNA at the house," Connor argued. "Don't know why anybody'd wait two years."

"We only have his word that the relationship ended two years ago," Gregory remarked. "*If* there was a relationship at all. And, if there was, Claire might have ended things more recently, which could have been the reason."

The other men fell silent while they considered his words, then Niall spoke again.

"I've ordered a second tranche of lab testing," he said. "It'll cost us—a heck of a lot—but this can't go on. I want all the old samples re-tested, and some we disregarded the first time."

"Disregarded?"

"It's the way of it," Niall explained. "We don't have endless resources, so we need to prioritise samples that look the most promising. We sent through what was found in the doorway, the hallway, the bathroom and the child's bedroom. We held off sending through what we took from the other communal areas."

"What about the back fence? Where there's a gap?"

"We didn't find anything there," Niall replied, and then caught Gregory's expression and sighed. "I'll ask them to check again."

"How long will it take for them to come back?"

"Usually, it takes weeks," Connor said. "But the mayor's approved some financing from the town's emergency fund. We'll order the express service, which can come back in anywhere from forty-eight hours to a week."

As they entered the Garda station office, they found a visitor waiting for them.

"Inspector—Niall?"

Liam Kelly stood up from one of the low-backed, folding chairs arranged in the tiny entrance foyer. He was a man of thirty-eight but appeared to have aged at least ten years over the past month—his skin was pallid and unshaven, his eyes bloodshot, and he was dressed down in jeans and a woollen jumper which told them he hadn't attended church that day.

They could hardly blame him.

"Liam," Niall stepped forward to take the man's hand in both of his own, while Gregory watched with interest. "How are you holding up?"

The man's eyes immediately began to water.

"Just the same," he managed, and looked across at Gregory. "I wondered if there'd been any developments?"

"Why don't we have a seat?" Niall said.

He curved an arm around the man's shoulder and led him through to a side room set up as a 'Family and Friends' area, presumably for the conveyance of bad news, judging by the pamphlets on bereavement and counselling strewn across the coffee table beside a jumbo-sized box of Kleenex.

Gregory followed them inside and shut the door behind him, then turned to face the blunt edge of grief.

"I thought you'd be able to tell us who did it."

Liam Kelly looked Gregory in the eye and dared him to respond.

"It doesn't work that way," Alex said, gently. "I look at the facts and the evidence, the geography of the town and its residents. Most of all, I look at Claire, to see why anybody would want to hurt her. I compare her murder with others I've seen before, to see if there are any patterns of behaviour that might help us to understand the nature of her killer, so the Garda can focus their attention on the sort of person most likely to fit the bill."

"Alex is here to give us the benefit of his experience," Connor added. "We've never had to deal with anything like this before. We needed a specialist."

Liam nodded miserably and sank into an overstuffed chair.

"Claire's still gone," he whispered. "Even if you catch him, she'll still be gone."

"We're doing all we can," Niall said. "Believe me—"

"I know you are," Liam mumbled, and ran his hands through his hair, to keep them occupied. "Some of the family are getting angry and impatient—and sometimes I feel it, too. But I know you're doing your best. In my heart, I know you wouldn't let me down."

Niall stood up and paced to the wall, where there was a large notice board filled with outdated posters advertising karaoke nights at O'Feeney's, and sunshine yoga classes down by the lough.

Place was turning into a bloody tourist trap, he thought, and felt a powerful urge for a drink.

Just a quick slug, to take the edge off.

"We think it's somebody in Ballyfinny," he said, and swallowed to ease the dryness in his throat. "We wanted to believe it was an outsider, but now we're not so sure."

Liam's eyes burned with anger and disbelief.

"Somebody she knew? No. No, I can't believe—who?" He shook his head, answering his own question. "Nobody we know could have done that to Claire."

It was the same instinctive reaction the Garda men had felt, but they had to face the facts, and so did he.

"I'm sorry, Liam. We were blinded to the possibility, because we didn't even want to think it," Niall said. "But we have to think it."

"Did Claire change her routine at all, in the weeks leading up to her death?"

Gregory's question came out of the blue, and served to distract Liam from his devastation, if only for a moment.

"Um, no. Not as far as I can remember. She tended to stay in the house on Saturday mornings, while I took Emily to her swimming lesson. She did most of the nursery pick-ups and whatnot during the week, so I liked to do my bit at the weekend and give Claire some time to herself. She usually had a bath and read a book, or pottered around the house or in the garden. She was always there when we came back."

His voice broke on the last word, and Gregory could feel Niall's warning look boring into the side of his face. They had not discussed the matter of Claire's alleged affair, yet.

But they must, and soon.

"How were things between you? Did Claire seem happy or was anything bothering her?"

Liam clasped his hands between his knees.

"She was happy, or seemed that way," he said. "We had a baby on the way, and she was nesting. Started on at me to clear out the spare room and paint it. The only thing she seemed bothered about was getting everything ready for the little one."

He smiled at the memory.

"I was a bit worried about money," he confessed. "But not enough to speak to her about it. We would have been fine."

He fell silent, retreating into himself as he replayed the final days of their lives together.

"How's your daughter coping?" Gregory asked him, once again diverting the man's thoughts towards something tangible, real and—most importantly—very much alive.

"She keeps asking when Mammy's coming back," Liam said, and covered his eyes. "I don't know what to tell her. I want to say she's gone to Heaven, with all the angels, but I can't see past the last image of her, lying there on the bed. I can't see her anywhere else."

"We need to help you to replace that image with a better one," Gregory said. "A happier one, that you can associate with Claire whenever you think of her."

"I don't know if I can."

"You must," Gregory told him. "If not for yourself, for your daughter. She needs your strength, and she needs to be able to talk openly about losing Claire. If she can't, if she's too afraid of hurting you, it'll be harder on both of you in the years to come. We need to help you to replace the final image of Claire in your mind, so that whenever she's spoken of, you can visualise her in happier times."

Liam brushed a thumb beneath his eyes, hardly aware that tears had leaked from the corners. "I want to," he admitted. "I want to be able to think about her without my stomach churning. I see Emily watching me, asking questions…"

"Where did you ask Claire to marry you?" Gregory asked.

Liam was surprised.

"Ah…it was down at the Cliffs of Moher, south of Galway. I took her there to see the ocean. It was a perfect day," he said, wistfully.

"You should think about taking Emily there—take the family, too. Celebrate Claire's life, relive a special moment and remember her as she was, then. Share it with your daughter, don't squirrel it away in the recesses of your mind."

Liam looked over at the quiet Englishman and wondered what it must be like, to step inside the shoes of another person and know precisely what to say, and how to say it.

He stood up to shake Gregory's hand.

"I appreciate the time," he said. "I'll speak to Emily today, and start planning a trip."

Gregory returned the handshake.

"It's a good, positive step."

Liam nodded, then turned to the Garda.

"While we're gone—"

"We'll still be here," Niall promised him. "We won't forget, Liam."

Once he'd left the station to make his way home to his daughter, Connor turned to Gregory and put a hand on his shoulder.

"I know you said you couldn't work magic, but that was a good imitation."

CHAPTER 16

Hearing Liam Kelly's grief first-hand had not come as a surprise to Gregory, since he dealt with grief in all its forms as part of his training and practice. However, it never got any easier. There were no pro-forma words he could say that would help the living who remained; only instinct, and a willingness to listen. Contrary to Connor Byrne's belief, there was no magic involved, and he didn't get it right every time.

You couldn't win them all.

Sitting in the little 'Family and Friends' room at Ballyfinny Garda Station, with its stale air and peeling paint, Gregory had called upon some advice he'd once received from a murder detective in the North of England; a man by the name of Ryan, who dealt with the worst of humanity every day and seemed to wake up each morning still thinking the best of the world and those who inhabited it.

"Follow your conscience," Ryan had told him. *"Never tell the family any lies, but don't rob them of hope, either. Hope's sometimes all there is."*

Now, as he stood in front of the Murder Wall, he wondered when Claire Kelly's killer had lost all hope. When had the connection between them and the rest of society broken down so irretrievably that killing one of its number seemed the best way to expel the darkness they harboured inside?

Was it hate that had driven them to it, or a crooked form of love?

He knew that the staging of her body was significant. It had been, from the very beginning. But did it speak of love or of hatred—even jealousy?

Perhaps, as with so many of his patients, there was no 'clever' reason to it. They'd simply had the will and the drive to kill, and nobody would ever understand why.

Gregory shook his head at that.

His every instinct as a clinician told him there was a reason behind the killer's choice; something important and, at present, known only to them. The Garda had taken his advice and, over the coming days, they'd agreed to re-evaluate the movements of the town residents. They would begin with those in Claire's inner circle, moving gradually out to those she seldom had any dealings with, in order to narrow the pool of potential suspects with means and opportunity. He had his own list, tucked away in his jacket pocket, and it would be interesting to see if it matched the one the Garda produced.

After all, his list contained the names of two of their number. Neither Niall nor Connor Byrne had provided statements for the file, and nobody had pressed them on it.

But he would.

"I meant to ask," he said, turning to Niall. "With the divisional office being based in Castlebar, what made you stay living here in Ballyfinny?"

Niall was hunched over his computer, but he looked up and leaned back in his chair, stretching his hands above his head to ease the kinks in his back.

"It's home," he explained, getting up to wander across the room, where an old-style coffee machine churned out caffeinated sludge. "We grew up here. My Ma has Declan most Fridays and she sees plenty of us through the week, so she'd miss that. Family's important to her."

He gestured with an empty coffee cup and Gregory nodded.

"Thanks."

Niall started up the coffee machine, which made a sound not dissimilar to a spacecraft taking off, then leaned back against the counter to wait.

"Emma's family is here too," he continued. "I should say, her mum is. Her dad passed away not long ago."

"I'm sorry," Gregory said, automatically.

"Cancer," Niall pulled a face. "It hit her mum hard, so Emma goes over to visit whenever she can to help out around the house and all that. Her Ma's not like mine; Maggie Byrne can handle most things— and has done, over the years."

Gregory could have played dumb, but he preferred to be direct.

"I was sorry to hear about what happened to your father," he said.

Niall battled the usual feeling of impotent rage that washed over him every time he thought of it, then the coffee machine let out an ear-piercing *beep* to signal its cycle had ended. He poured brownish water into two mugs, one bearing a faded Leprechaun, the other a map of the lough and an emblem of a four-leaf clover.

"Here," he said, handing the one with the Leprechaun to Gregory. "Maybe it'll bring us luck."

Gregory took a sip, then winced.

"Yeah, it's not exactly Columbia's finest," Niall chuckled. "But it does the job."

"Who does the job?" Connor asked, as he stepped back into the Major Incident Room with a file tucked under his arm.

"This does," Niall said, raising his cup. "The Doc and I were talking about why I stayed in Ballyfinny. Truth is, Emma and I never should have left Dublin. We were happy there, when I was at the NBCI and she was doing her teacher training."

"Ah, now," Connor said, dropping the file on his desk. "You're both country folk. You'd have missed these hills, all the way over in Dublin, surrounded by all the traffic and strife of the city."

Niall stared into the bottom of his cup.

"Maybe," he muttered.

Gregory watched their byplay and, armed with his newfound knowledge of their family history, realised that it was their mannerisms, not their looks, that were so similar.

He took a fortifying sip from his cup, then grasped the nettle.

"When I was going through the statements in the file, I noticed yours were missing," he said, smiling at both of them. "Can I have a copy of each, please?"

The brothers looked at each other, then at him.

"You think one of *us* would do that, Doc?" Connor was affronted.

"He's covering all the bases," Niall said. "As we should have done. It's not personal, Con."

He turned to Gregory.

"It's a shock to have the shoe on the other foot, that's all," he said, easily enough. "I'll type up a statement for you tonight, but I'll tell you here and now: on the Saturday Claire Kelly died, I was at home all morning. Emma went to collect Declan from Ma's house, and the two of them were home by eleven."

Gregory turned to Connor and waited.

"I don't believe this," the man muttered, then held up his hands. "Fine, *fine*. I was right here, on duty at the station."

"With anybody?"

Connor swore roundly.

"No, b' Jesus, I was on my own—as I've a right to be, as a grown man."

Gregory's face remained impassive, and Connor shifted uncomfortably.

"There wasn't anybody else on shift, if that's what you mean. Before all this happened, Ballyfinny was just a quiet town. The worst we ever deal with is the odd bit of poaching or theft of farm machinery. It doesn't take a squad of Garda officers to deal with that, so I was on my own."

Niall turned to his brother with interest.

"Did you take any calls?" he asked.

Connor shook his head.

"There was only one call, that morning, and it came from Liam Kelly."

Gregory thanked them both, and wondered if Niall Byrne would have the strength to check the phone records for incoming calls to Ballyfinny Garda Station.

He kept both men on his list, for now.

CHAPTER 17

As the day drew to a close, Gregory stood on the steps of the Ballyfinny Castle Hotel with his bag at his feet and looked out across the lough. It was Big Sky Country, he thought; the kind of place that reminded you of how small you were, in the grand scheme of things. In his case, he was just one man standing beneath a blazing sky knowing that, somewhere out there, another soul may be looking up and feeling the same insignificance.

He heard the crunch of tyres on gravel and spotted Maggie's car approaching along the winding driveway. With impeccable timing, Seamus came out to greet his sister and to see him off, while Padraig materialised from somewhere within to snaffle his bag and load it into the boot of her car before he had time to say, 'hands off'.

The hand was definitely quicker than the eye, in his case.

"Ready?" Maggie called out, and, with a final word of thanks to the general manager and his concierge, Gregory folded his long body into the passenger seat of her compact Fiat.

"Might've known you'd have a tiny car," he complained, to make her laugh.

She let out one of her legendary hoots, then gunned the engine into life, swinging into an elaborate U-turn before heading off in the direction of the airport.

"Seamus hates it when I turn around in front of the hotel like that," she said, wickedly. "It leaves indents in his perfect driveway."

Gregory gave a lopsided smile, glad to see she hadn't lost her sense of fun, despite everything.

It was a thirty-minute drive back to the airport but, rather than subjecting him to her favoured radio channel, Maggie fell into conversation.

"How've you found the trip?" she asked, and he smiled again.

What she really wanted to know was: how had he found *them*? Her people, her family and friends in the town.

He answered the unspoken question, to set her mind at ease.

"You couldn't have prevented this," he said, as the car swept through the thick woodland surrounding the hotel. "It could have happened to anyone, anywhere in the world."

Maggie turned the car onto the main road, slowing to a snail's pace as they were caught behind a slow-moving tractor whose driver was clearly in no rush to be anywhere fast.

"It plays on my mind—all times of the day, but especially at night," she said. "I keep wondering whether there were signs I should have seen. Odd behaviour I should have noticed. There just wasn't."

"Don't blame yourself," he said. "The only person responsible for what happened to Claire Kelly was the person who took her life."

Maggie was silent for a few minutes, until the tractor turned off the road and she was able to accelerate once more.

"I was thinking about what you said, the other night, about them being broken and needing help," she continued. "Part of me *hates* to think that, because I don't *want* to pity them, Alex. I don't want to care about them, not after what they've done to Claire and her family."

"That's understandable," he reassured her. "It doesn't make you a bad person."

"I know. But I was thinking about how these killers, or rapists, or whatever they may be, usually have some awful trauma in their childhoods. Terrible experiences that shape them into these broken-down adults."

Gregory nodded.

"There are various schools of thought," he said. "But, as far as I'm concerned, killers are not born. They're *made*. That doesn't mean to say that everybody who suffers childhood trauma will grow up to be a killer. If that were true, half the known world would be locked up at Southmoor."

She flipped on her lights as dusk began to fall, and the dashboard illuminated her profile, which was set in lines of worry.

"Seamus told you about what happened to Aiden," she said, and her voice wobbled a bit. "It's been over thirty years and it still hurts to think of it."

Gregory broke with his own rules, put a hand on her shoulder and gave it a quick, supportive squeeze.

"Thanks," she said, huskily. "I wasn't at home, the night it happened. People didn't have mobile phones back then, so the first I heard of it was when a knock came on my friend's door. I was around there, laughing about some nonsense or other, while Aiden was dying with Niall there to see the whole thing."

Gregory gave her a few moments to recover, then picked up the thread of conversation.

"You're worried it's affected him," he said, cutting to the heart of the matter. "Niall suffered extreme childhood trauma, for which you're blaming yourself—again—and you're worrying…What do you worry about, Maggie?"

Her lips trembled in the reflected light of the dashboard, but she shook her head.

She would not bring herself to say it.

She would not even think it.

"I told you Niall and Emma are having some trouble at the moment," she said. "They haven't told me exactly why, and I don't want to pry. All I know is, Niall's drinking is getting worse. You saw what he was like, last night."

Wisely, Gregory chose to remain silent.

"I've tried talking to him, but he tells me there's nothing to worry about," she said. "Back then, in the eighties, things weren't as developed as they are now. There were no counsellors and few child psychologists that people trusted. We saw it as a community problem; something we'd deal with, together."

"And did you—deal with it, I mean?"

Maggie shook her head again.

"I did my best," she said. "The family rallied around, and he was never without a friend to play with, but there were times…"

She trailed off, and Gregory frowned.

"What times, Maggie?"

"With animals," she said, tremulously. "I got a dog for Niall and Connor to look after, when they were little. I found it poisoned in the back garden."

Gregory spoke with extreme care.

"Are you sure it was Niall?"

Maggie opened her mouth, then shut it again.

"I-I always assumed. He spent the most time with it, so I thought—I thought it must have been him."

"Boys who suffer abuse inside an orphanage are just as vulnerable as those who witness their father's murder," he said softly. "They're also equally capable of healing, with the right kind of loving mother to guide them. Like I said, not everyone who has a difficult childhood grows up to be a killer, Maggie."

She parked the car and rested her hands on the steering wheel. When she glanced across at him, there were tears in her eyes.

"Thank you," she said, with feeling. "I think I owe you a consultation fee, after all that."

"You owe me nothing," he assured her, and reached for the door handle. "I'll work on the profile this week and travel back next weekend. In the meantime, call me, if you need me."

Or, if anything happens.

He poked his head back through the door, as an afterthought.

"Look after your family," he said. "And don't travel anywhere alone."

If Maggie was frightened by the warning implicit in his words, she hid it behind a cheerful smile.

"Safe travels," she said, and waited until his tall figure had disappeared into the airport terminal before starting the car again.

Motherly instinct, she supposed.

CHAPTER 18

The air smelled of iodine.

It was all around him; in his hair, crawling over his skin, and inside his mouth, like black smoke. He coughed and spluttered, his lungs bursting as he tried to find his way through the misty haze, to the fresh air beyond.

Alex ran mindlessly through empty streets, his footsteps clattering against the cobblestones, until he came to the edge of a steep bank. He tried to stop, but suddenly he was falling through the air, his body lurching forward as he plummeted through empty sky and into darkness.

There was a sickening *crunch* of flesh and bone as his body hit something hard and cold, but he felt no pain. Lifting himself onto his knees, Alex found he was inside Ballyfinny Abbey, at the foot of the altar. Above his head, a golden effigy of Jesus Christ was suspended, tears of blood weeping from his painted face and onto the floor, where it ran in small rivers towards where he kneeled.

When he looked up again, it was not the son of God who looked down upon him but a pale-faced woman with a gaping wound in her heart.

Alex scrambled away and turned to run, but found the path was blocked, and the doors barred.

Six children stood in a row in front of him, their skin almost translucent in the candlelight. The eldest boy held a small puppy in his hands, his serious young face stained with tears. A little girl in pink pyjamas clutched a teddy bear in her arms and held the hand of a little boy with bony arms and legs. Behind them, a shadow approached, dressed in a dark cassock.

"*I am death,*" it said. "*Come with me, now.*"

But it was not the priest.

It was Cathy Jones.

───────

Alex woke in his own bed, on the south bank of the River Thames.

He'd chosen to live in the city centre because, no matter what the time of day or night, there would always be life outside his window.

A quick glance at the clock told him it was shortly after four a.m., so he rolled off the edge of the bed and walked to the window, throwing it open to the night air and the salty scent of the river. Comforting sound filtered into the room; a combination of late-night revelry and early-morning deliveries that made up the hum of city life.

Alex stood there for a long time resting his forearms on the window-ledge, letting the air cool his over-heated skin and calm his over-charged mind. He watched lights twinkling on the inky-black river and knew that, in another hour, they would be replaced by the dim glow of sunrise. His loft apartment was one of ten inside a renovated warehouse building from the Victorian era, in a popular, upmarket area of the south bank known as 'Shad Thames'. There were countless restaurants, bars, theatres and art galleries, offering plenty of opportunity for a single man of means to meet people.

He couldn't remember the last time he'd stepped foot inside any of them.

His friends were scarce and carefully-chosen; his work all-consuming. Romantic entanglements were a complication he generally avoided.

But he was no saint.

There had been women, in the past. Short-lived relationships that were more physical than anything else. There may be others in the future.

But there would never be a wife, or somebody to see him in moments of weakness, such as these. He'd made the decision many years ago never to entrust too much of himself into the hands of another, and there had been nobody to change his opinion on that score.

An image of a woman with long, red hair floated into his mind.

"I want her," he admitted to himself. "But not at any cost."

And the cost would be high, with that one. There were others to think of; children whose lives would be torn apart.

The answer was 'no'.

And so, he would continue to live a half-life; a purgatory of emotional deadlock, where he would step into the hearts and minds of others without compromising his own.

Bill Douglas had once told him he was like a chameleon, with an uncanny knack for being able to fit into any new environment, so that those who lived there might think he was one of them.

But he was not one of them.

He was something apart; an island inhabited by one, with an occasional visitor permitted very rarely to share his solitary life.

He did not belong.

He would never belong.

Gregory stepped away from the window and looked around the smart flat with its polished wooden floors and exposed brickwork, its glossy kitchen and plain white bedding. Everything was utilitarian, designed for a man who needed only a place to rest his head at night.

To his surprise, he found tears on his face, and he scrubbed them away with an angry hand.

Time to get back to work.

CHAPTER 19

Tuesday
London, England

The week passed quickly at Southmoor Hospital, as Gregory slipped back into his routine of patients and clinical meetings during the day whilst, at night, he worked on the 'Ballyfinny Butcher' profile, which is what the press had decided to christen the person who remained dangerous and at large in the small Irish town. There was always a tension between those who reported the news, and those who sought to repress it, or control it—including himself and the police. The problem was compounded by a need for news to have an element of 'click-bait' nowadays; a requirement that the headline be sensational enough to draw in the punters, who might go on to purchase a toaster through some affiliate link and ensure the journalists' wages were paid at the end of the month.

Gregory understood it and regretted it, in equal measure.

In all the cases he'd seen, not one perpetrator of violent crime had complained about their being immortalised in the public consciousness—the opposite was true. Infamy gave some killers a reputation to live up to, driving them to top their own best efforts, again and again. It enraged others; shining a light on their private efforts, drawing them out when they would rather remain safely hidden in the shadows, quietly operating behind the scenes.

And, for some, it served only to legitimise their cause and glorify an otherwise painfully ordinary persona.

Gregory thought of all this, and more, as he rolled up his sleeves and began to chop red peppers for the frittata he planned to make for dinner.

The intercom buzzed, right on time, and he checked the camera.

"Come on up," he said, wiping his hands on a tea towel.

A minute or so later, Professor Bill Douglas puffed his way to the door. He was dressed in what Gregory thought of as one of his 'tweed specials', consisting of a heavily threaded jacket over brown chinos that looked as though they'd begun life in a thrift shop, topped off with a mustard-coloured scarf and flat cap.

"Lift's out of order," he said, wheezing a bit.

Douglas bestowed a manly hug before moving past Gregory to hook his hat and scarf on a peg in the tiny hallway.

"Still haven't put any pictures up, I see."

"You know I don't like clutter."

"There's uncluttered, and then there's 'Cell Block'."

Gregory grinned, then wandered back to the kitchen area where he began breaking eggs into a mixing bowl.

With the familiarity of long friendship, Douglas rooted around the fridge for a bottle of his favourite beer, then settled himself on a barstool to watch.

"You look tired," he said. "You've not been sleeping, again."

"Thanks, Dad."

Douglas was undeterred.

"Tell me about it."

Gregory began to beat the eggs with a whisk, thrashing the inoffensive gloop with unnecessary force.

"The profiling case is playing on my mind," he said. "I think I know the killer's motivation, but I can't be sure without another death. Even then, I don't know how the profile will help the police."

Douglas heard the frustration in his young friend's voice and was sorry for it.

"Start at the top," he suggested. "What's the motivation?"

"I think the killer *coveted* Claire Kelly, or what she represented. They wanted it for themselves, to keep, and the only way they could do that was by removing her from the world."

"And, *de facto*, from everybody else," Douglas said.

"Exactly."

"What did she represent?" Douglas wondered. "An attractive, unattainable young woman?"

There had been many cases of inadequate, sexually repressed men seeking out women they admired from afar.

"That was my first thought," Gregory said. "But I lean more towards her role as a mother or caregiver. It fits the staging of her body."

Douglas made a low sound in his throat as he considered the ramifications.

"On the child's bed, with a teddy and a storybook?" he recalled. "Yes, I see what you mean. You think whoever killed her coveted her role as a mother?"

"Not the role, as such," Gregory said. "I'm not sure whoever killed her harbours feelings of inadequacy about their own motherhood; in fact, statistically, her killer is more likely to be male. It would have taken some strength to do the heavy lifting, too."

"If not the role itself, then what?"

"I think they wanted her, and everything she embodied, for themselves; as a replacement or proxy for something they lacked, or still lack."

Douglas took a long, thoughtful swig of his beer.

"Do you think it's a one-off killing, or do we have a Keppler situation on our hands?"

He referred to the infamous American serial killer, Ed Keppler, who killed several women as proxies for his own mother, who he worked up to killing before ultimately handing himself in to the police.

"I honestly don't know," Gregory admitted. "There's some suggestion that the victim had an extra-marital affair, which complicates things. The police are beginning to lean towards the ex-lover, who doesn't have an alibi for her murder. If they're right, and I'm wrong, he might have killed Claire as a one-off, for more straightforward reasons—but it doesn't fit with the staging of her body. A jealous ex-lover doesn't kill in that way, after a delay, unless something precipitated the attack."

He paused.

"Claire Kelly was pregnant," he added.

"Might've been the lover's baby," Douglas said, reading his thoughts easily. "But that's pure conjecture. You have to focus on the facts."

"I agree, which is why I've suggested that the Garda—neither of whom have a satisfactory alibi themselves—turn their attention to building a list of suspects from the local area, focusing on those whose movements are not accounted for."

"Do you believe the police are involved?" Douglas asked.

Gregory thought of how they'd sought to repress material facts relating to Tom Reilly, apparently on compassionate grounds, and could not rule out the possibility of more serious collusion.

"The two detectives handling the investigation are brothers—not by birth, as it turns out, since one of them was adopted. Both suffered childhood trauma, and their mother is the town mayor. She told me on Sunday night that she suspects one or both of them were responsible for killing a family pet, when they were children. It's textbook."

"Strong, authoritarian mother figure, you mean? Aggression towards animals leading to escalation in later life, perhaps?"

Gregory poured the egg mixture into a pie dish and set a timer on the oven door before answering.

"Maggie Byrne is a nice woman," he said, reaching for a glass of wine he'd poured earlier. "But she could be perceived as authoritarian from an internal, family-dynamic perspective. Neither of her sons would dare to argue with her, I think. That's the kind of subtle repression that can drive people over the edge."

Douglas blew out a gusty breath and rolled the beer bottle between his hands as he thought back over all the cases they'd worked on, in the past.

"And, beneath all this, let me hazard a guess and say you're nervous about putting forth a profile based on so few evidential facts."

Gregory gave a brief nod.

"Alex, what happened the last time wasn't your fault or mine," his friend said. "There was a public witch hunt, and the police needed a couple of fall guys to explain why an innocent man was sent to prison. We were available and fitted the bill."

He paused, then shrugged philosophically.

"Do we really begrudge it? The police do a good job, most of the time, and not all of them have the training to deal with the trauma of what their job entails. They're told to get results, then they're hung out to dry when things go wrong."

"I know," Gregory nodded. "But it's taught me caution."

"Maybe too much caution?"

Gregory swallowed a mouthful of wine and was annoyed to find another image of Emma Byrne popping into his mind's eye.

He frowned.

"There's a woman," he said, deciding he may as well off-load the lot. Douglas was one of the few friends he allowed into his life, but he was also his professional supervisor and mentor. "She's the wife of one of the police officers, and the mayor's daughter-in-law."

"You sure can pick 'em," Douglas joked, and wriggled his preposterous eyebrows. "What's her name?"

"It doesn't matter," Gregory said, irritably. "The point is, I'm worried about her. She's a mother, in a town where another young mother has recently been killed. If I'm right about the killer coveting women like her, she could be in very real danger."

"You're focusing your concern on this woman because you're attracted to her," Douglas said, cutting to the chase. "Is there any reason to believe she would be targeted more than any other mother in the town, if that's the killer's motivation?"

Gregory knew he was right, and said as much.

"I feel sorry for her," he realised. "Her husband isn't a bad man, but he's got his own problems and their marriage is failing."

"And, then, you come along," Douglas said. "A handsome stranger, with healing hands."

Gregory couldn't prevent the laugh that bubbled in his throat, but then his smile faded.

"Do you ever resent the professional duty that comes with the job?" he asked. "The knowledge that, no matter how tempted you are, you're precluded from ever acting on your impulses? In a normal world, when men and women meet, they make their own decisions without having to abide by a rule book."

Douglas heard the yearning in his friend's voice, the pain of longing, and wished there was a cure for loneliness.

"Of course, I've felt that way," he said quietly. "I practised for many years, and there were times my restraint was tested. When that happened, or when I was concerned there may be a breach in the doctor-patient relationship, I relinquished the patient and passed them on to one of my colleagues."

"This woman isn't a patient," Gregory muttered.

"Isn't she?" Douglas countered. "Aren't they all patients, when you're profiling? The whole town is in need, so the whole town deserves your duty of care."

Gregory nodded slowly, and the oven timer began to let out a loud beep.

"Time's up," Douglas smiled, and raised the beer to his lips.

CHAPTER 20

Thursday
Southmoor Hospital

A couple of days later, Gregory was still ruminating on the discussion he'd held with Bill Douglas, when the door opened to admit his final patient of the day. Cathy Jones entered the room with a confident stride, dressed to the nines in her smartest clothes and having taken the time to paint every inch of her face.

His heart sank.

He had grown adept at recognising her mercurial moods, and one look was enough to tell him which version of 'Cathy' he would be treated to that day.

"Good afternoon, Doctor," she said, sliding down onto the sofa in a slow, languorous movement. "I've missed you, this week."

"Hello, Cathy," he said, in a clipped tone. "How have you been?"

"Lonely," she said, pouting a bit.

He referred to the printed schedule in her file.

"I see here that you've done a lot of group work, this week," he reminded her. "Art and music… gardening, too. It sounds like you've had plenty of company."

She snorted.

"They're all mad," she said, without sarcasm. "If I spend too much time with them, it'll start to rub off. I'd rather be alone than have to listen to some of their ravings. Loneliness really depends on *whose* company you have, or don't have—wouldn't you agree?"

The muscles in his jaw clenched so hard, he heard a crack.

"Today, I thought we could talk about what happened after your daughter Emily was born," he said, pleasantly. "You've told me before that it was a difficult time for you."

"I don't feel like talking about that, today. I want to talk about *you*," she said, leaning forward to toy with one of the tissues from the box on the coffee table. "You know, I've always loved green eyes, just like yours. Do you have a girlfriend, Alex?"

He folded his hands and looked at her for a long moment, battling a strong sense of revulsion. It was as though Cathy was a child or a teenager, trapped inside the body of an ageing woman. How could it be that she had mothered three children, and killed two of them? She looked at him now with such wide-eyed innocence, a lesser man might have doubted what his eyes and his ears told him.

"I've warned you before, Cathy. Our relationship is a professional one, and nothing more. I'm here to help you to understand yourself better, and help you to heal. My personal life is entirely outside the bounds of that relationship, and I'd appreciate it if you didn't ask me again."

Her mouth turned sulky and hard.

"You're a *fag*," she spat.

His eyes flashed a dangerous warning, while he kept himself under rigid control.

"Watch your language," he said. "And modify your attitude."

"Alright, it's because you think I'm old enough to be your mother, isn't it?" she taunted him. "What's the matter, sweetheart? Can't handle an older woman? Worried that I might know more than you do, is that it?"

She leaned back on the sofa, cackling to herself.

"I've had most of the male nurses in this place," she said. "One of them told me he loves me."

Some of the pity must have shown on his face, for she suddenly erupted in anger.

"Don't you look at me like that!" she screamed. "I know what you're thinking! You think I'm lying, just like you think I'm lying about the children! I'm telling the truth!"

Her face contorted, and he braced himself for an attack, unsure whether she would lash out or cry.

It wouldn't be the first time.

When she crumpled into floods of inconsolable tears, he closed his notebook and called for Pete, the security liaison nurse, who was stationed at his post just outside.

He entered within seconds.

"Everything okay, Alex?"

"Fine, Pete. We're done here, for today. Could you escort Mrs Jones back to her room, please? I hope you come to the next session with more willingness to participate, Cathy."

As she was led away, she hurled obscenities at his back, spitting and snarling like an alley cat. In the silence that followed her departure, Gregory thought of the nightmare he'd had earlier that week, where she'd made an appearance as an Angel of Death.

It's what the press had named her, before her trial at the Old Bailey.

With every session, he hoped to unlock that part of her mind that held the elusive answer as to why she'd done it; why she'd spooned salt into her baby's bottles, why she'd malnourished and mistreated her children until another one became so ill that he died, and another barely survived.

But, as with so many who suffered from factitious disorders, he feared Cathy would never tell him the answer to those important questions. There would be no rehabilitation for the woman so long as she cosseted herself in deep denial, unable to admit to her crimes and unwilling even to try.

He wondered whether the same would be true of the person who had killed Claire Kelly. Would they ever learn what impetus had led them to kill?

Perhaps, after all, Maggie Byrne was right.

What difference did it make to know the reasons, when the result was the same: a woman was dead and wasn't coming back—just as Cathy Jones' children were long gone, their lives lost in the sands of time along with so many others.

CHAPTER 21

Despite his doubts, Gregory stationed himself at his desk and read over the working profile he'd put together for the Ballyfinny case. It was a lengthy document, so he'd created a summary which covered the main points:

PSYCHOLOGICAL PROFILE
OFFENDER: A.K.A. "Ballyfinny Butcher"
Victim(s): Claire Ann Kelly (29) and unborn child (2.5 mth gestation)
Ballyfinny, Co. Mayo, Ireland.
Police liaison(s): Inspector Niall Byrne (Divisional Head, Co. Mayo Garda, Castlebar); Sergeant Connor Byrne (Head of Garda Station, Ballyfinny).

In compiling this profile, I have considered all available information made available to me from the crime scene (including location, staging, time of day and year) and have analysed any available forensic data drawn from the physical evidence, which has been scant. I have read and considered all available witness statements, as well as secondary statements that were taken by the police more recently and the autopsy report prepared by the pathologist. Additionally, I have considered the type and manner of assault prior to death, geophysical factors, logistical means and personality traits of the victim that may have been relevant to her relative 'risk'. If further evidence comes to light following the submission of this profile, it will be updated accordingly.

This profile contains a list of personality and behavioural characteristics of the offender, as well as a suggested sequence of events leading to the victim's murder. This has been compiled by reference to established research into criminal behaviour and personality types, as well as qualitative analysis of patterns revealed in other like crimes. The profile should be used by the Garda to help narrow their list of potential suspects. Please note that it does not conclusively generate or eliminate suspects. The Garda should focus their attention on suspects who fit the profile, in the first instance, but never close their minds to the possibility of an outlier.

Sequence of events
The autopsy report states that CK died between the hours of eight-thirty and ten-thirty, which is an unusually specific approximation of post-mortem interval, made possible by the fact her body was discovered very quickly after death

occurred. *Information taken from the victim's family reveal her husband, Liam Kelly, left the family home at approximately eight-fifteen, taking their young daughter to the swimming pool in the nearby town of Ballina for a nine o'clock lesson. The journey took him approximately thirty minutes both ways, allowing for time to get changed etc. and was a regular weekly occurrence. The Kelly home is located at the end of a country lane in an isolated position, not directly overlooked by any neighbours, and is accessible from the front or the back, as there is a public footpath through woodland to the rear of the property, giving access to their back garden. No physical evidence was recovered from either the windows or the doors to indicate forced entry, and CK sustained an immobilising blow to the back of the head once she and her assailant were inside the house, suggesting her killer was able to gain entry and knew CK would be alone.*

The location and timing of events strongly suggests her killer had advance knowledge of the fact CK would be alone in the house; information that could have been readily available given the close-knit community setting but is more likely to have been confirmed by the killer in a series of visits, where he/she observed the Kelly family's routine. Taking into account the careful staging of CK's body in her daughter's room, which has a wide window offering a clear view to the back garden, it is my view her killer observed CK with her daughter on several occasions in that room and therefore used the public footpath at some point. However, on the day CK died, they came to the front door. Whilst it is possible the killer was unknown to CK and was able to gain entry through nefarious means, it is more likely that CK knew or trusted her killer and invited them into her home.

The autopsy report, blood spatter patterns and evidence of large-scale blood loss in the bathroom is consistent with the Garda theory that, following a blow to the head using a heavy ornament taken from her hallway, CK was dragged to the bathroom, where she was moved into the tub and dealt a killing blow using a knife with a blade approximately five or six inches long, as yet unrecovered. This is significant on two counts: first, the killer may have brought their own weapon for the killing, but was not concerned to bring a weapon to immobilise. This may be because he/she was confident that, without a weapon, they were of superior physical strength and could have immobilised CK without it, but it is more likely because they were familiar with CK's home and knew there was a heavy bronze ornament on the hallway table that they could use. Second, the killer was not squeamish or afraid to face his/her victim.

For there to be little or no DNA evidence found at the victim's home, her killer exercised extreme caution, which demonstrates careful and organised premeditation rather than a crime carried out in the heat of the moment. It is likely they brought a change of clothes or coveralls and gloves, as well as the duct tape used to seal the knife wound. For the sake of completeness, I should mention that the following persons, whose DNA was found in the Kelly home because of a pre-

existing relationship with the family/being a member of the Garda's First Response Team, should not be discounted:
Garda Team
Forensic Team
Garda Doctor / Local GP
Wider family of CK and LK
Friends of CK and LK
Tom and Kate Reilly (see appendix note).

The offender dealt CK a single, killing blow to the heart, which is significant not only because of the emotional connotations associated with matters of the heart, but because it is a difficult organ to penetrate and would have required significant force and strength of nerve. Most first-time offenders experience panic and demonstrate clumsy methodologies, however this method indicates confidence, some knowledge of anatomy and strength to deliver the blow. The killer's choice of this method may indicate one of two things: a personal dislike of CK and desire to punish; or, a desire to use CK as a proxy for some other significant person in the killer's life. Taking into account the care the killer took to clean and re-dress the body, comb CK's hair and arrange her on the bed, and the absence of more 'frenzied' knife wounds, it is my opinion that her killer falls into the latter category.

Following the staging of the body and a thorough clean-up of all communal areas in the house, CK's killer might have exited via front or back, but most likely front, given the absence of any prints or physical evidence recovered from the adjoining pathway.

Personality and behavioural factors

CK was, by all accounts, a non-confrontational person and generally passive by nature. This elevates her associated 'risk' as a suitable proxy for her killer's purposes, since she was less likely to fight/run/cause commotion, and tells us that the killer is more comfortable and confident selecting a victim of that category.

Her killer was organised, capable of planning and self-restraint, although this will diminish so long as they remain undetected. This behaviour makes it more likely he/she is able to sustain gainful employment, relationships and standing in the community. It is also less likely they demonstrate 'obvious' behavioural traits associated with unstable behaviour. However, the Garda should consider prioritising suspects who have suffered life-altering trauma, which may have precipitated one of two things:

a one-off psychotic break, leading to the planning and execution of the attack on CK; or,

a historic break, causing the development and escalation of long-term aggressive behaviours (e.g. towards animals, children etc.) leading to eventual planning and execution of the attack on CK.

In general, killers who seek proxies as substitutes for the 'real' person they would like to kill continue to escalate as they grow in confidence and move closer to their 'real' target.

(N.B. if the 'real' target is already dead, a killer may continue to use proxies indefinitely until their dissatisfaction leads them to make errors, commit suicide or, alternatively, hand themselves in to police). In this case, it is my view that the killer coveted CK's role as a mother/primary caregiver and was conflicted in their desire to 'capture' her essence, whilst also removing CK from the world, insofar as she represented a person for whom they harbour resentment (either justified or unjustified)—namely, a mother figure. I do not believe CK's killer demonstrates psycho-sexual motivation at present, but this may develop as feelings of power are associated with the taking of life. This is borne out by a lack of semen or other bodily fluid found at the crime scene.

The killer is able to blend in within the community. In previous cases, offenders have belonged to 'unseen' professions, e.g. postman/woman, as well as more prominent, 'trusted' professions, e.g. doctors, teachers, religious leaders. For this reason, the Garda should focus on suspects in public service or retail occupations within the town, or alternatively in prominent and trusted local positions, e.g. church, town council, school, paying close attention to work patterns and logistical availability to commit the crime.

The physicality of the victim and method of killing would suggest an able-bodied male assailant...

Gregory leaned back in his chair and stretched his arms above his head, surprised to find it was growing dark outside. He rubbed his eyes and reached across to flick on the desk light, whose eco-friendly bulb shone a thin white-grey light over the scarred wooden desk and bore an uncomfortable resemblance to those found in the hospital mortuary, two floors below.

The profile may be meaningless, he thought; a jumble of words and thoughts that bore no resemblance to the person they eventually apprehended.

On the other hand, it might contain something that could help.

He typed a final sentence at the end of the summary, then clicked 'SEND'.

As Gregory was locking up his office for the night, he was approached by one of the ward nurses.

"Alex? Do you have a minute?"

"Of course," he said, shifting his briefcase to his other hand as he pocketed an enormous keyring. "Anything the matter?"

The nurse looked harried, her nerves frayed around the edges.

"I hate to trouble you, as you're on your way home," she said. "The thing is, we can't get Cathy Jones to settle down. She says she won't sleep without her rosary."

He shook his head.

"You know the rules around personal effects," he said. "That includes religious paraphernalia."

"But, surely, since she's been here so long—"

Gregory interrupted her, speaking urgently.

"It doesn't matter how long she's been here. Cathy Jones remains a danger to herself and others. Have you read her notes?"

The nurse nodded.

"Then you'll know the previous attempts she's made to escape, and to attack nurses and doctors responsible for her care. She's *unpredictable*. She can't be trusted with anything that could be fashioned into a weapon."

He was deadly serious, so much so that the young nurse took a half-step away.

"Don't turn your back on her," he warned. "Never, *ever* turn your back on somebody like that."

He waited until the nurse had relayed his decision, and then moved along the corridor to Cathy's room. A Perspex glass window facilitated twenty-four-hour observation, and he peered through the glass to find her kneeling beside the single bed, which was pushed against the side wall and drilled to the floor.

Her hands were clasped together, and her mouth moved in silent prayer.

He imagined what she might be saying, or asking of God to forgive, and was reminded of what Father Walsh had told him about the sanctity of confessionals. If Cathy Jones was making her confession, he did not belong there.

Alex moved away again, as silently as he had come.

CHAPTER 22

Friday

While Alex Gregory steeled himself to board the tiny plane from London to Knock Airport for a second time, Colm McArdle zipped up his jacket and poked his head around the living room door.

"I'll be off now, Aideen," he said. "I won't be late tonight, my flower."

She looked up from the novel she was pretending to read, and snorted.

"That'll be the day," she said. "Didn't you tell me the same story, last week?"

"Aye—but, you know, Ned Malloy had a birthday…"

"Oh, for pity's sake," she said. "Lord save us from all the birthdays and anniversaries you and those no-goods you call friends seem to have every Friday night."

He grinned at her.

"That's why I fell in love with you," he crooned. "It's an intelligent woman you are, Aideen."

She snorted again, and louder this time.

"Only in comparison with you, Colm McArdle," she quipped. "Now, be off with you, if you're going, and leave me in peace."

But she was pleased when he trotted over to bestow a kiss, which she returned wholeheartedly. They hadn't enjoyed so many years as man and wife without having a little bit of spark between them.

"Save those kisses for me," he said, with a wink.

"I'll save them for Cillian Murphy," she muttered, and fiddled with the remote until the latest episode of *Peaky Blinders* appeared on the small television set in the corner of the room.

The novel forgotten, she settled back with a contented sigh and reached for the small bag of fruit gums she'd hidden beneath her knitting bag.

The journey over the Irish Sea to Knock Airport was no less death-defying than the last time, and it turned out that forewarned was not necessarily forearmed when it came to the impact of gravity upon one's internal organs. Consequently, Gregory's stomach was still settling back into its usual position as he walked through the automatic doors leading to the arrivals area, where he expected to find Maggie Byrne or Padraig waiting for him, as before.

It was neither.

Emma had been leaning against one of the pillars, the toe of her boot resting back against the concrete. When she spotted him, she raised a hand and waved him over.

Gregory had no way of preventing the small burst of pleasure it gave him to know that she'd come to meet him. It took only a few seconds to close the distance between them but, in that time, he drank in the sight of her. She was dressed simply in black jeans and a matching jumper, against which the bold red of her hair rippled like liquid fire beneath the industrial lighting overhead. She wore scuffed boots and carried a raincoat over one arm.

"Hello again, Doctor Gregory."

"Alex," he said. "I was expecting to see Padraig."

"Sorry to disappoint you," she said, with a smile. "His Land Rover has finally packed in, and Maggie's looking after Declan tonight. Besides, night driving is hard on her eyes, so I offered to come instead."

"Thanks," he said, as they stepped out into the chilly evening air. "Where's Niall, this evening?"

She looked over at him, then away again.

"He's out," she said, and crossed the short-stay car park towards a small blue SUV. "This one's mine. The boot's full of junk, so just sling your bag on the back seat."

He did as he was told, his eye falling on the child's seat and the small collection of books littering the back of the car. He took a deep breath before tugging open the passenger door.

She was a good driver, handling the car with easy confidence as they made their way through the quiet countryside towards Ballyfinny. Gregory watched her hands on the wheel, then looked away, out of the window at the passing night.

There was an uncomfortable silence.

"I—"

"Are—"

They spoke together, then laughed.

"You go first," Gregory said.

"I was going to say, 'Are you sorry to be back in Ballyfinny?'"

He watched the way the headlights of passing cars lit up her face and hair, and knew the answer to that question was simple.

"Yes," he said. "And, no."

She glanced across at him and smiled.

"You're one of those complicated types," she said. "I can tell."

"Am I?"

"All men are," she qualified. "It's in your genetics—I'm certain of it."

"There must be some research, somewhere," he said, angling his body towards her. "But I thought we were simple creatures."

Their eyes met briefly, before she turned back to the road ahead.

"Niall's a complicated man, too," she said, and slowed the car at a sharp bend. "He's been working all the hours, on this case."

"He's dedicated," Gregory said, and swallowed something

in his throat. It might have been guilt. "I hope he finds my profile useful."

"He's talked of little else," she said. "He and Con have been putting together fresh lists of suspects to look at more closely, based on your ideas. He says you've got a knack for stepping inside people's minds."

Gregory said nothing.

"It must be a lonely place," she said softly. "I wouldn't want to roam inside anybody else's mind; I'd be afraid of what I found there."

"I'm not afraid," he said. *But it can be lonely,* he added silently.

They were silent for a few minutes, each content to watch the road ahead, and then she took a sudden turn to the left, pulling the car to a standstill along a narrow country track.

"Is everything alright?"

She unbuckled her seatbelt and turned to look at him.

"I need to tell you something," she whispered.

Colm McArdle polished off the last of his pint, then checked the time on the antique clock hanging above the bar in O'Feeney's.

Nine-fifteen.

He'd promised faithfully that he'd be home at a reasonable hour, and b' God, he meant to keep it. "Another half, Colm?" his friend asked.

He warred with himself, caught between the friends he'd known since boyhood, and the wife who'd give him the cold shoulder if he pushed his luck.

"Aye, why the devil not? It's early, yet."

The table cheered him on.

"A round of the Black Stuff!" Colm told the barman.

"Aideen'll be in here, wanting my guts for garters," he said. "I took a tellin' from my grandma, last week, for serving you past ten o'clock."

"Ah, now. Would you begrudge an old man his bit of pleasure?"

The barman laughed.

"On your own head, be it!"

Colm scooped up the glasses and wound his way back to the table beside the fire, where the conversation had turned to murder.

"Awful, *awful* thing," one of them was saying. "And she, nothin' but a girl."

"Knew her grandfather," another one said. "Good man."

At that moment, Padraig stepped into the bar, and they raised a hand in greeting.

"A pint for our friend," Colm called out to the barman, and cleared a space for the newcomer. "He's got the look of a man with a terrible thirst."

The men laughed, and Padraig joined them.

CHAPTER 23

In the moments following her declaration, Gregory waited in expectant silence, wondering what Emma planned to say, and how he might react, when she did.

"Before I tell you, I want you to know I'm not proud of myself," she said, eventually.

He asked the necessary question.

"Are you speaking to me as a psychologist, as a criminal profiler, or…as a man?"

She looked across at him, her eyes tracing the lines of his face, and swallowed.

"There's a lot I'd like to say," she admitted. "But what I have to tell you now is…I think it's for the profiler."

He nodded, and refused even to acknowledge the nagging, demeaning sense of disappointment that settled in the pit of his stomach.

"I'm listening."

"It's about Tom Reilly," she said in a rush. "I heard Niall and Con talking about how he had an affair with Claire a couple of years ago. That's true."

He waited for her to tell him how she knew.

"Claire told me first, but Tom…he told me, later."

Gregory's face remained impassive.

"You're not saying much," she burst out.

"Neither are you," he replied, and she let out a nervous laugh.

"It's hard to find the words," she said, in a thick voice. "But the way things are going…I heard Niall say he's going to be looking harder at Tom, because he doesn't have an alibi for the Saturday when Claire died. He thinks Tom was over there, killing her, but he wasn't."

She looked him in the eye.

"Tom was with me, that Saturday morning. He told his wife he was going for a jog, and I told Niall the same."

A shutter fell across Gregory's eyes, and she noticed.

"I'm sorry," she muttered. "I'm so ashamed."

"Why are you telling me this, and not your husband?"

She wiped away tears, and he produced a tissue from a small pack lying on the back seat, near Declan's box of books.

"Thanks," she muttered, and blew her nose. "I'm telling you, because I trust you and I don't know what to do for the best. Things have been bad between Niall and me for a long time now, and his drinking keeps getting worse. I don't know where he goes, some nights…"

"He's a Garda detective," Alex argued.

"And his brother is, too. Not to mention his mother, the mayor," she said, leaning back against the car seat. "They're a close family."

"But not you?"

"I regret what happened with Tom, but he's a kind man, and one of the uncomplicated ones," she said, with a sad smile. "Neither of us are terribly happy, and we needed to be close to someone. Can you understand that?"

Yes, he thought. *He understood only too well.*

"It's material evidence," he said quietly. "You have to give a statement to the police."

She turned to him.

"I will, but please don't say anything to Niall. Not yet. If he's still convinced Tom's involved in a couple of days, I'll tell him myself. We've been trying to work on things, for Declan's sake. This will crush him."

Gregory looked away from her, and out across the dark fields.

Only days ago, he'd lectured them about the ethics of withholding Claire Kelly's affair with Tom Reilly from the official file. Now, he was considering the same action himself, and for similar reasons.

"Do you mean to stay with him?" he asked.

She hesitated, and then nodded.

"So long as his drinking doesn't get any worse...yes."

A muscle ticked in his jaw, and he rubbed an absent hand over the skin.

"We'd better be getting back," he said. "Your husband will be wondering where you are."

Colm McArdle stumbled out of O'Feeney's bar shortly after ten and congratulated himself on his remarkable self-restraint. He whistled merrily as he walked the short distance home, a route he had taken almost every Friday for the past forty years, at least. He waved to those he passed but didn't stop; eager now to get back to the woman he knew would be waiting for him in the comfort of hearth and home.

At the end of the street, he paused to look up at the moon, which was full and bright.

"That's a pretty thing," he muttered to himself, and continued along the pavement.

When he reached the cottage, a quick peep through the window told him that, although the living room was in darkness, a light still burned in the kitchen.

"There's a rare woman," he mumbled to himself, as he reached for the door handle.

His Aideen wouldn't leave a light burning for him, unless she was in a forgiving mood.

Inside, the hallway was dim, and he fumbled for the light switch on the wall. He spent another five minutes untying his shoelaces, a task made much harder by his sudden inability to balance himself.

With a muttered curse, he toed off his shoes and hung his coat on the stand in the hallway.

"Aideen?" he called through to the kitchen. "Be a love and put the kettle on?"

Colm relieved himself in the downstairs cloakroom and, yawning widely, shuffled through to the kitchen.

Aideen was seated at the kitchen table, with her back to him. At first glance, she seemed to be sprawled in the chair with her neck at an awkward angle resting on her chest, and he assumed she must have dozed off, while she was waiting for him to return.

She'd even set out the tea things, so they could have a bite of supper together.

Funny, he thought, the little habits they made together.

"Come on now, girl, let's get you up to bed," he said, though he could barely hold himself upright.

He moved forward and dropped a light kiss on the top of her head, which caused her to slump further in her chair.

"Aideen?"

He put his hands on her shoulders and tried to shake her awake, but her arms seemed frozen in place.

Through the haze of alcohol, he saw that they'd been taped to the arms of the chair to keep her in place.

With shaking fingers, he cupped her beloved face in his hand and lifted it to the light.

"*Aideen*," he said, brokenly.

The remainder of the journey to the Ballyfinny Castle Hotel passed in silence, with Alex and Emma each lost in their own thoughts. However, as the car pulled up to the entrance, she made a small sound of surprise when she spotted a squad car parked outside.

"The Garda's here," she murmured, and sent Gregory a nervous look.

Ignoring her, he slammed out of the car and retrieved his bag, intending to head inside. Then, at the last moment, he turned to face her across the length of the bonnet.

"You have to tell Niall," he said. "Not just because honesty is important for your ongoing relationship—which it is—but because another man's life could be seriously affected if you don't. If Tom Reilly has an alibi, the Garda need to know about it."

She nodded.

"I know you're right. I think it's why I came to you, because I knew you'd tell me to do the right thing. I'll speak to Niall—"

She was cut off by the arrival of his brother, who ran out of the hotel entrance with a face like thunder.

"What the hell took you so long?" Connor said, but didn't bother to wait for a response. "We need to get back into town, *now*."

"Why? What's happened?" Emma asked, and put a hand to her throat. "Is it Maggie? Declan?"

Connor shook his head.

"It's neither. Emma, you go on home now. Alex, you're with me."

Gregory didn't need to ask why; the answer was written all over the sergeant's face.

There'd been another murder.

CHAPTER 24

When they turned into the street where Aideen McArdle
had lived for most of her life, it was teeming with people
craning their necks and chattering like magpies. In the rear-
view mirror, they saw a white, nondescript van pull up, and
a man and a woman jumped out carrying heavy television
cameras. Up ahead, a small cordon had been erected around
the entrance to a cottage at the end of the street, manned by
two young guards who were trying to hold back the tide.

"Christ," Connor muttered. "It's a circus."

He turned to the man beside him.

"Prepare yourself," he said. "It's bad, in there."

Gregory nodded, though it wasn't the first time he'd seen
death, and probably wouldn't be the last.

"Do you have spare coveralls?"

Connor nodded.

"Everything's in the boot," he said. "I keep plenty of spares
in there."

As soon as they exited the car, the television crew spotted them and hurried over to try to catch a scoop.

"*Sergeant! Sergeant, is it true the Ballyfinny Butcher has struck again?*"

"No comment," Connor growled, elbowing them out of the way so he could reach for his safety gear. "Move out of the way, before I do you for obstruction."

"*Doctor Gregory? Have you provided a profile to the Garda? Are you planning to re-open the Profiling Unit?*"

When he looked back, he was startled by the blinding white light of a television camera, and raised a hand to shield his eyes as another flash popped nearby. Gregory said nothing, keeping his head down as they moved through the gathering crowd towards the cordon.

"*Sergeant? Is it true the Garda have no leads? Did Doctor Gregory's profile prevent an arrest being made before now?*"

Connor swung around, prepared to defend their consultant, but Gregory shook his head. His skin was thick enough to take whichever darts were thrown and, besides, there were more important matters at hand.

They hurried past, ignoring the shouts from reporters, and ducked beneath the cordon. Connor scrawled their names in a logbook to record those entering and leaving the crime scene, then passed him some blue shoe coverings.

"Niall's already in there with the doctor and the CSI's," he said. "I've called in some more guards to get the crowd moving. They can't stay out here, all night—weather's turning cold, for one thing."

"Never underestimate the tenacity of a devoted rubbernecker," Gregory muttered, and tugged polypropylene coveralls over his jeans.

"Ready?" Connor asked.

Gregory looked at the tiny cottage with its novelty sign hanging by the doorway, which read, 'HERE LIVES A LOVELY LADY AND A GRUMPY OLD MAN'.

"Ready as I'll ever be," he replied.

When they entered the McArdle house, Gregory almost stumbled over the crouched figure of a Crime Scene Investigator, whose eyes were the only thing visible behind their protective face mask and hood.

"Sorry," he said, and stepped carefully around, keeping to the plastic sheeting that had been laid out for them to walk on. Behind him, more CSIs went about the business of erecting a small tent around the doorway to preserve any evidence before the elements washed it away.

"Through here," Connor said, and they made their way towards the kitchen at the back of the house. It had been built along similar lines to Maggie's, with a living room at the front, a kitchen-diner and small downstairs cloakroom towards the back. Upstairs would be a bathroom and larger master bedroom, with a second smaller bedroom and a third box room, if they were lucky.

They paused on the threshold of the kitchen while the forensics team snapped a series of photographs, studying the shell of Aideen McArdle from every possible angle.

Life, laid bare, Gregory thought. Only hours ago, the old woman slumped in the kitchen chair had been a living, breathing thing; she'd developed complex layers of personality and emotion and harboured many thousands of memories in her hippocampus and prefrontal cortex.

Now, only the shell remained.

"Alex, Con, you can come through now," Niall said, and beckoned them inside.

Their coveralls rustled as they walked into the room, leaving a wide berth around the kitchen table where two senior CSIs picked over the body with swabs and brushes.

"Aideen McArdle, aged seventy-three," Niall said, in an odd, emotionless voice. "Born here in Ballyfinny, married a local man by the name of Colm. Worked a bit here and there but she was a homemaker for the most part. They've children and grandchildren, as you'd expect."

Gregory angled himself to get a better view of the woman, and of the scene the killer had staged, but it was impossible with so many people milling around.

"I need to see it as the killer left it," he said.

"We took photographs," Niall offered, and then thought better of it. "I s'pose five minutes won't hurt."

He ushered the others out of the room, leaving Gregory alone with Aideen for a moment. Without other bodily odours to mask it, he could detect the first, subtle hint of decay; a sickly-sweet, unmistakable smell unlike anything else.

"How long has she been dead?" he asked, as he studied the duct tape wrapped around the woman's swollen flesh.

"Doctor thinks no more than two or three hours," Niall said, stepping back into the doorway. "She was still warm when her husband came home at around quarter-past ten. The pathologist is on her way from Galway, she might be able to give us a better estimate."

Gregory checked his watch.

Eleven thirty-five.

Aideen's body had been taped to one of the wooden chairs arranged around a circular kitchen table so that she remained upright. The right side of her head bore an ugly wound, matted with crusted blood, and a small bloodstain seeped through the front of her dress, roughly where her heart would be. At some point, she might have held a cup in her hand which had since fallen to the floor, where it lay in a drying pool of weak tea-coloured liquid.

"Have the CSIs sampled the teapot and the kettle?"

Niall nodded. Even the most careful of killers could forget to wipe the edge of a handle—or the tap.

On the table, tea had been set for two. A pot stood in the middle, beside a plate of jam tarts Aideen had made that morning.

"What was used to immobilise, this time?"

"CSIs bagged one of the copper pans," Niall replied, and his suit rustled again as he raised a hand towards a set of heavy-looking cookware hanging from a rack on the wall above the cooker, near the back door.

"Another knife wound to the chest?" he asked, and the inspector nodded.

"No sign of the knife, before you ask."

When Gregory said nothing, Connor moved forward.

"It's a different kind of victim, this time," he remarked. "Different age group, too."

"They weren't so different," Gregory replied, skirting around the table to look out of the kitchen window. "They were both mothers, for one thing. Both nurturing character types."

He lifted a finger to the window.

"What runs along the back of the garden, here?"

Niall moved over to join him beside the window and looked out into the night.

"There's a pathway running behind the fence," he said. "Every garden has a gate leading out onto it, and if you follow the path west, it'll take you to the lough, past the cemetery. Follow it north and you go past the school and into the centre of town."

"Easy access," Gregory said. "Just like the Kelly house."

"There's more chance of being noticed around here," Connor argued. "You saw for yourself how nosy folk are on the street."

"Only for things out of the ordinary," Gregory said. "Remember, we're looking for somebody who fits in and is part of the tapestry, here. Nobody would notice if they saw this person walking by and, even if they did, they might not recall or think it was worth mentioning. There's another thing to consider, in terms of the killer's choice of location: this is the last house on the row, so it'd be easy enough to slip along the pathway and let yourself in via the back door."

"It's due to rain overnight, but the CSIs will get as much as they can from the garden area before morning comes," Niall said.

"They watched her." Gregory turned back to look at what had once been Aideen. "They saw her in here, having tea with her family, and wanted to capture the feeling for themselves and bottle it, somehow."

"Sick bastard," Connor said. "What about the profile? You think this is the same person?"

Gregory nodded.

"Highly likely. The details of the last murder weren't made public, so that reduces the chances of a copycat looking to try their hand. The body has been meticulously cleaned and dressed," he said. "I'll bet you find the modus operandi is the same, with one exception. The Kelly house was one-storey, whereas the bathroom's upstairs in this house. The killer couldn't carry Aideen's body up and down the stairs to wash and dress it. They must have found another alternative."

"Downstairs cloakroom has a small shower area," Niall provided. "The McArdles only installed it recently, as they were starting to struggle with mobility getting in and out of the bath upstairs. The CSIs are taking the shower apart, now."

Gregory looked at the other two men, his face set in a hard line.

"The killer couldn't have planned Aideen's murder without being local," he said. "There's no other way they'd have known about the new shower, for one thing."

This time, neither of the Garda detectives argued the point.

CHAPTER 25

Saturday

It was after midnight by the time they finished their initial survey of the crime scene, and later still by the time Alex and Niall stopped into the attractive, modern two-storey house owned by Colm McArdle's daughter, Lisa, and her family.

"He'll be staying with them here, tonight," Niall said, as he brought his car to a stop at the end of her driveway. "I rang ahead and spoke to the son-in-law, who tells me the family want to see us tonight. I told them it could wait, but—"

"They need to hear it from you," Gregory said. "They know what's coming, but they still need to hear it. It's part of the process."

Niall nodded, and, by tacit agreement, Gregory joined him on the walk to the front door. He watched the inspector draw in a deep breath and arrange his features into something akin to a blank canvas, before raising his hand to knock.

It was answered within seconds by Colm's son-in-law, a thin man with sad eyes and a prematurely balding head.

"Come in," he said, holding the door open. "They're waiting for you in the living room."

Colm was surrounded by five other people when they stepped inside, one of whom was Maggie, who looked exhausted but relieved to see them. Another was Father Walsh, who wore a perennial look of acceptance. There was a family liaison officer Connor had appointed to stay with Colm and his family; Colm's daughter, Lisa; and the fifth was a person Gregory had never seen before.

Father and daughter were seated on the sofa, their hands clasped tightly together. The old man's skin had an unhealthy grey pallor and his eyes had the unfocused look of one suffering from extreme shock, while his daughter's face had been ravaged by tears.

"Mr McArdle?" Niall stepped into the room and perched himself on the edge of one of the remaining chairs, while Gregory remained standing just inside the doorway.

When he made no response, Colm's daughter rubbed a gentle hand over his arm to stir him.

"Dad? The inspector's here. Maggie's boy—Niall?"

Colm blinked, trying to focus.

"Niall?"

"That's right, Mr McArdle," he replied. "I'm so sorry for your loss."

Gregory had spoken to many police officers and detectives over the years, and none of them relished this moment, which was surely the worst part of their job. He knew the feeling, from times when he had been required to call the families of patients who passed away, and did not envy Niall his task.

"Where's Aideen?" Colm asked. "Where's my Deenie?"

"In a higher place," Father Walsh said quietly. "A better place."

Unaccountably, Gregory felt a surge of anger, which he swiftly repressed.

"We're looking after her body, Colm. We'll take good care of her," Niall said. "Now, what's this I hear, about you not wanting to go to hospital for a check-up?"

The fifth man was apparently a doctor, and he leaned forward to reiterate his advice.

"You've had a terrible shock," he said. "I'd like to keep you under observation, just for tonight, and tomorrow morning we could re-assess."

Colm nodded, his head bobbing up and down like a puppet, but it was clear he wasn't listening.

"I told her I'd be home early," he said, robotically. "I told Aideen that."

"You weren't to know this would happen," his daughter whispered. "There's no way you could have stopped this."

"I broke my promise," he continued, and his hands began to tremble. "I should have been there with her. I should have—"

"This isn't your fault," Maggie said, in a voice thick with unshed tears. "I'm so sorry, Colm. We're all so dreadfully sorry."

"Every Friday I was gone," he muttered. "Why did I do it? Why did I ever leave her, even for a minute?"

"It was normal, Da," his daughter said. "You can't blame yourself."

"They could have had me," he whispered, and tears began to leak from his eyes. "Why didn't they come for me instead?"

Gregory's heart ached because he knew that, if Colm had been there, Aideen's killer wouldn't have followed through with their plan. Nor would they have taken him, instead; whoever had set up Aideen's macabre tea party was seeking a fairy tale mother, or grandmother—not a father.

"She was the prettiest girl in all of Mayo," Colm whispered, and began to shake, his body suddenly convulsing back against the sofa.

"He's in shock," the doctor said, rushing forward. "Clear some space!"

They fell silent, watching as he helped Colm onto his back and instructed his daughter to elevate his legs to increase blood flow. They kept their distance while he worked, checking heart rate and pulse, all the while speaking to Colm in a calm tone that seemed to have been patented by doctors the world over.

But then, the tone changed.

"Call an ambulance," the doctor ordered. "He's going into cardiac arrest."

Colm McArdle passed away before the ambulance arrived, in the arms of his daughter and in the presence of his priest, who administered the last rites.

News spread quickly that fresh tragedy had befallen the town, and it didn't take long for the vultures to descend. Men and women with white, camera-ready smiles stayed late into the night and returned before dawn, circling around an already crippled town, ready to snatch whatever scraps they could find.

"Haven't they got homes to go to?" Connor muttered, from his position beside the window in the Major Incident Room.

It was shortly after six o'clock, and the town was awakening to find another pillar of its community murdered. Canvassing of the local area had begun the night before, with sleepy-eyed guards going door to door, taking statements from Aideen's neighbours and the people she had called friends.

Many of them had seen Colm heading out for a dose of his Friday night medicine at O'Feeney's, but none had seen a stranger loitering outside, or a madman roving the streets, because it was as Gregory had already predicted: the person they sought was invisible. Claire and Aideen's killer breathed the same air as the rest of the community; they ate and drank, walked and talked like everybody else.

Just then, the outer door opened. Gregory looked up from where he'd been poring over a stack of mail and transcripts of telephone calls the Garda had received since Claire Kelly's death, each from some poor, desperate soul claiming to have been the one to kill her. Pitiable they may be, but their 'confessions' were brazenly inaccurate and bore no resemblance to the crime, so he set them aside as the Mayor entered the incident room carrying a plastic shopping bag.

Maggie was dressed all in black and her face was drawn into tight lines of anger which, to Gregory's surprise, seemed to be directed towards him.

"Have you seen this?" She set the plastic bag on top of a desk and lifted it upside down so that several daily newspapers fell out, hot off the press.

Gregory reached across to turn one of them around, and frowned when he read the headline:

"PROFILER CALLED IN AS BUTCHER STRIKES AGAIN."

A photograph, taken outside the McArdle house the previous night, captured him with his hand raised in what appeared to be an aggressive stance. Beside that image was an old, grainy photograph of the man who had been falsely imprisoned three years earlier, following a long-running investigation into the murders of male sex workers in London's Soho district. He skim-read the article, which was a re-hashing of the tabloid view following that case, and a thinly-veiled suggestion that his presence in Ballyfinny was little more than a cynical ploy to rebuild his reputation as a leading profiler, trading off the grief that was rife in that small town.

"What's the matter, Ma?" Niall asked, and crossed the room to see for himself.

Gregory passed him the newspaper with a steady hand, and faced Maggie with eyes that were like chips of green ice.

"Do you really believe that self-interest was my motivation in coming here?" he asked. "That I'd be so ambitious, so *narcissistic*, as to put my own reputation ahead of the wellbeing of people whose lives have been ruined—ahead of those that have been taken?"

Maggie realised quickly that she had spoken in haste.

"Alex—"

Gregory merely shook his head. If she was going to hurl accusations, he'd damn well exercise his right of reply.

"My work as a psychologist is the most important part of my life. Much more important to me than profiling killers. Do you think I *like* it?" he asked. "Do you think I like having their shadows crawling around my head at night, or images of the dead permanently imprinted on my mind?"

He lifted a hand and pointed towards her sons, who had the grace to look abashed.

"I don't do this for kicks," he said, with some disgust. "I do it for the same reason you do: to prevent further loss of life, and to bring some sense of justice to those who remain. I do it on my own time, unpaid, because I believe I can make some sort of difference. If there's even the smallest doubt in your mind concerning my reasons for being here, I can be on the first plane back to London."

The Mayor reached for the e-cigarette she kept inside her jacket pocket and took a long, healing puff of the minty fluid.

"Well, hell. There's no need to get your knickers in a twist," she muttered, and shuffled her feet. "Look, I don't often say this, so I'll do it quick."

"Say what?" he prompted.

"I'm sorry, Alex. That's what."

"I bet that hurt," Niall remarked, and his brother laughed.

"Not as much as your ear will, when I clip it," Maggie warned him.

"I mean it," Alex said quietly. "If I'm trespassing here, I have my own work to go back to—"

"You're not," she said. "It's been a bad few weeks, and last night was the worst, by far. My phone's been ringing off the hook all morning with journalists looking for a sound bite, town councillors and whatnot asking for progress updates and complaining about the press coverage. I don't have anything to tell them, and I guess it got on top of me."

She turned to look at her sons.

"I heard rumblings from a few of them about calling in the NBCI to take charge of the investigation," she said. "Patience is wearing thin."

"Hold a press conference," Gregory suggested. "Be a leader and show them you've got it covered. Send a message to the killer that you're redoubling your efforts, and leaving no stone unturned."

"How do you think they'll respond to that?" Connor wondered.

Gregory thought of the killer's behaviour, so far, and of their quiet comings and goings.

"I think it'll force them to exercise caution, or go underground, for the time being," he said. "They'll have the next person in mind, or will likely be looking around for them, but it might force them to stay their hand until things cool down a bit. At the very least, that buys you some time to get the DNA results back from the lab."

Niall nodded his agreement.

"It makes good sense," he said. "I want us to keep ahead of the press. Let's give them something proactive, rather than leaving them to print yesterday's news."

Maggie nodded.

"I'll set it up," she said.

CHAPTER 26

While Maggie Byrne fought political fires, the Garda set up an urgent briefing.

The station house in Ballyfinny was too small to accommodate all the personnel required to attend and the larger station in Castlebar was a forty-minute drive away, so they decided to commandeer one of the conference suites at the Ballyfinny Castle Hotel, which was by far the grandest setting for a murder briefing Gregory had ever had the fortune—or misfortune—to attend.

After a quick shower and change, he took up a position near the door.

"Habit of yours?" Connor asked, coming to stand beside him.

"What do you mean?"

"You like to be near the door," the other man said, giving a light shrug. "You plannin' to make a quick getaway?"

Gregory looked away, feeling slightly unnerved.

He'd grown so used to *making* behavioural observations, it came as a shock to be on the receiving end. Until now, nobody else had noticed the little quirk he'd developed over the years, especially as it was only a small thing and easy for most people to overlook.

Not for the eagle-eyed man standing next to him, it would seem.

"Ever been trapped in a room with one of the inmates?" Connor asked, as Garda staff swarmed into the conference area and settled themselves on gold-painted chairs normally reserved for wedding banquets.

"We don't call them inmates, but, yes, I have," Gregory replied, and thought of Cathy Jones.

"Touch that door handle, and I'll let go," she'd said, whilst balancing herself on the extreme edge of a chair, her fingers tucked beneath a noose she'd fashioned from torn bedsheets.

It had taken ninety minutes to talk her out of it, he recalled, and when he'd finally left the room, he'd vomited until there was nothing but acid left in his stomach. Acid, and the burning shame of knowing that a part of him had wanted her to die. Even while he'd talked her out of it, employing every trick he knew to keep her alive, the deepest, darkest part of his heart had hoped his efforts would fail.

Connor watched some indefinable emotion pass across Gregory's face, and decided not to press it.

"Briefing's about to start," he said, and left to join his brother at the front of the room.

Casting his eye around, Gregory could see officers from all tiers of the Garda hierarchy, as well as various people he guessed were support staff or members of the forensics team. At the last minute, an attractive, statuesque woman with a sleek blonde bob flashed her warrant card and slipped into the back of the room. Precautions had been taken to ensure no errant reporters found their way inside, and all personnel were required to show their badge before the doors were closed.

Niall clapped his hands and waited while conversation died down.

"I want to thank you all for turning out," he said. "It's a hell of a way to spend your weekend."

There were a few murmurs of assent.

"You're here because there's a killer amongst us," he said. "Worse than anything we've seen in a good long while—not just here, but in the whole of Ireland. There's no political or gang-related motivation that we've found, nor does there seem to be a sexual motivation, but we can't be sure on either count because the killer leaves nothing of themselves behind. No blood, no fingerprints, no DNA that we've been able to use."

He paused, gathering his thoughts.

"Contrary to what the press have started calling him, the 'Butcher' isn't really a butcher at all. It's our view that the murders of Claire Kelly and her unborn child, and of Aideen McArdle were perpetrated by the same person. It's also our view that this person planned the murders, probably weeks or months in advance, and executed their plans with precision. There was little or no blood found, either at the scene or on the victims' bodies, which were cleaned with a careful eye for detail after the killer dealt one immobilising blow to the head, followed by a single knife wound to the heart. These were no frenzy attacks, they were premeditated crimes."

One of the officers raised a hand.

"Is there any connection between the victims?" she asked.

"Aside from being resident in the same town, where they were casual acquaintances but shared no immediate family or friends, they were both female, both married homemakers and both mothers."

"Have you ruled out a copycat?" another one asked, and Niall shook his head.

"It's too early to rule anything out," he said, "but it's looking very unlikely that Aideen McArdle's murder was committed by a copycat—the MO is much too similar. That said, we'll wait to hear back from the lab to see what they find in the way of forensic evidence, and take things from there."

"You said nothing useful was recovered from the Kelly house," one of the sergeants from Castlebar put in. "If that's the case, what do you hope to recover from the McArdle house?"

"Anything would be welcome," Niall admitted. "But, you're right. If it's the same person, I don't expect we'll recover much. Not only will they employ the same methods as before, they'll refine them so our job will be made even harder."

"How do we catch them, then?" one officer asked. "How do we catch them, if we have no leads?"

Niall glanced towards Gregory.

"We've been working with a criminal profiler, as you might have heard. Doctor Gregory has a lot of experience in that area, and has come up with a profile of the sort of person we're looking for, to help us to narrow down a pool of suspects. Initially, we thought we were looking for an outsider, but it's clear that detailed knowledge of the victims and the local area would have been necessary. Coming to terms with that has already helped us to refocus."

To Gregory's dismay, Niall then turned and beckoned him forward.

"I'd like to ask Doctor Gregory to come forward and explain some of the key elements of his profile, so you can all have a better understanding of what we're dealing with, here. Doctor?"

Fifty heads turned to look at him, and Gregory knew when he was beaten.

———

"What you have to understand is, 'serial' or 'signature' killers are like you and me."

As Gregory might have predicted, that sent a few feathers ruffling around the room.

He held up a hand, calling for order.

"What I mean is, the person committing these murders is a hunter, just like us. We're hunting them, and they're hunting the people they see as 'prey'. We're trying to understand them and their motivations so we can bring them in, and they're trying all the while to understand their victims' lives, so they can come up with the most efficient way to kill them. It's two sides of a coin."

"But why pick Claire or Aideen?" one person asked. "Why them, and not someone else in the town?"

Gregory tucked his hands into the back pockets of his jeans, and wondered where he'd picked up that particular habit.

Certainly not from his father, who would never be caught dead wearing jeans.

"These victims ticked the right boxes for the killer," he replied. "Their homes were suitably isolated, so the killer could move freely without being rushed. They were vulnerable; either as an expectant mother or as an older person who was less able to run away, or because of their own tendency towards introversion."

"Speak English, Doc!" one of the support staff called out, sending a ripple of laughter around the room.

Gregory flashed a quick smile and tried again.

"I mean to say, they were shy. Less likely to put up a fight."

"So, he likes the vulnerable ones," Connor said. "How does that help us find him?"

"How the killer behaves mirrors their personality," he said. "In the case of Claire Kelly, their choice of location and timing indicates that they were risk-adverse. They knew she'd be alone for several hours and the chances of discovery or interruption would be low. Likewise, in Aideen's case, they knew she was likely to be alone for several hours, but they couldn't be sure. There was always an outside chance that

Colm would break with tradition and come back early. The location was also a little riskier, being closer to the centre of town. That tells me the killer had grown in confidence, whilst still demonstrating a fundamental aversion to risk-taking. Factor in the nature of the crime and the lack of ultra-violence, and you begin to build up a picture of a killer who's submissive, careful, and just a little cowardly."

"Cowardly?" Connor gave a funny half-laugh. "It takes some guts to pull off what this guy's done, doesn't it?"

"Not really," Gregory replied. "In this case, the killer feels *compelled* to kill these women. It may go against their basic personality, which is probably non-violent and non-confrontational. The killer hasn't conducted a mass shooting, or held the town to ransom—at least, not in the traditional sense. They sneak around and, if they were ever interrupted, would be more likely to run than to stand and fight."

"You said they feel 'compelled'. What exactly do you mean by that?"

This last question came from the blonde woman at the back of the room. When some of the other officers heard it, Gregory noticed they sat up a little straighter in their chairs.

Apparently, the boss was on site.

"I mean that, by killing these women, the offender has reached a stage where their real life and their fantasy life have merged. In their real life, they're the easy-going, unthreatening character I've described; albeit they might have sought a position of relative power in their professional life, to compensate for a lack of it in their personal one. This overriding feeling of repression, or a lack of personal power or autonomy, probably developed in childhood. To deal with it, our killer built up a powerful fantasy world in which they imagined things being very different. That fantasy world has slipped over into reality, and they were no longer able to separate the two."

He paused, thinking of the crime scenes with their teddy bears and tea sets.

"I think we have a killer who wants to be a child again," he said quietly. "They covet the 'perfect' childhood and, in particular, the 'perfect' mother. Perhaps because they had neither, at least in their own perception of things."

"And so, they're killing these other women because they happen to be mothers out of—what?" she asked. "Jealousy, or spite?"

Gregory shook his head.

"I don't believe it was either. Looking at the killer's treatment of the bodies and the time spent arranging things, I believe our killer liked them—maybe even *loved* these women, enough to crave spending time with them and to create a fantasy scenario where they were the child. The only way they felt they could do that was by killing them."

There were more murmurs around the room as the Garda tried to wrap their heads around the idea of one person being capable of living two different 'realities'.

"Why now?" Niall asked. "If this all started when they were a kid, why have they only just started killing?"

Gregory shook his head.

"I've said before that I think the killer may have tried their hand in other, smaller ways; experimenting with violence," he said. "However, I believe it's possible that some recent traumatic event might have triggered the change, and now they're escalating."

"Because they've killed twice, now?" Connor enquired.

"Yes, but also looking at the location of the murders. Usually, a first murder or rape is committed further away from where a killer is based, although still within the catchment of what you could call their 'comfort zone'. They still know the area, but they don't like to shit on their own doorstep."

There were a couple of snorts.

"The Kelly house is located on the outermost edge of town, near the lough. The McArdle house is located on the other side of town, but closer to the centre. It's still reasonably isolated, being the last house at the end of the street, but it's not as far out as the first location."

"You think he's moving closer to home?" Connor asked.

"Possibly. Remember, I'm talking about what is *usually* the case; that doesn't mean it is *always* the case. Usually, a killer grows in confidence and starts to look for targets a little closer to where they live because they're more familiar with the area and its locale, the likely times they'll be seen, and so forth. It also allows them to slip out more regularly to stalk their intended target, without having to travel miles for the privilege."

He met Connor's eye.

"The threat of a Garda investigation hasn't deterred this killer. They've killed again, and more boldly this time, even knowing they're under scrutiny. Not only are they escalating, they're enjoying their first real taste of power, and power can be very addictive."

"We've already compiled a list of men and women who have no alibi for the time Claire Kelly was killed," Niall said. "We've narrowed that list into segments covering those who were free regularly on Saturday mornings; those who live within a half-mile radius of her home; those who knew or worked with her, and those who have any pops on their record, no matter how small. We've come up with a short-list of names of those who feature on three or more segmented lists."

Gregory nodded. It was good, solid police work, and exactly what they needed.

"If you can do the same for Aideen McArdle, we can see if there's any crossover between the two."

"Already started," Niall said.

Gregory smiled, but it was not because the Garda were taking positive steps in their investigation. It was because, for the first time since he'd met him, Niall Byrne bore the look of a man in command of the situation, and himself.

He only hoped it would last.

CHAPTER 27

Maggie arranged the press conference for noon.

It was to be held outside the Town Hall, which doubled up as the public library, the job centre, the citizen's advice bureau and general hub for any other public service you cared to mention. It also occupied a plum position overlooking the town square, right opposite O'Feeney's.

The founding fathers of Ballyfinny had obviously known that running the town was thirsty work.

Now, the small square held a crowd of locals and out-of-town reporters, who were jockeying for position at the foot of the stairs outside the Hall to see who could secure the best view while the Mayor made her address. Odds were even between the camera crews and parents wielding buggies; one could catch the back of your head, but the other could hobble you at the ankles.

Gregory had changed into a suit for the occasion—the only one he'd bothered to bring with him—and had encouraged the Garda to be in full dress uniform. It was important to send out a message of authority, not only to allay the fears of the wider local community, but to remind anybody else who might be watching that this was no game. As with Claire's funeral, offenders were often drawn to the media coverage surrounding their crimes, so there was a good chance her killer would either come to the press conference or watch it on the local news. On one level, they were probably following the coverage of their case because the idea of being important was exciting to them and, like Dorian Grey, they were enthralled by their own image, such as it was. It also gave them an opportunity to relive their crimes.

On another level, it was just good common sense.

At precisely twelve o'clock, Maggie and Niall took up their positions in front of the cameras, while Gregory stood at the back, next to Connor. He'd politely refused their request for him to make a speech; he was done with those, and it was best that any messages were conveyed by the town's own elected representative, who commanded respect.

"Thank you all for coming..."

Maggie was no longer a mother, or a grandmother, but a stateswoman. With a subtle shift in attitude and demeanour, her voice rang out across the square, striking a perfect note of candour and condolence. The killer had succeeded in dehumanizing the women they'd killed, and it was important to rehumanise them, so they would experience guilt for their crimes. For that reason, Gregory asked Maggie to mention Claire, Aideen and Colm frequently by name, and to speak of their family's devastation. They needed to remind the killer that their victims were not inanimate objects, but living, breathing human beings with hearts and souls. Only then might they begin to feel some remorse.

"*To Claire, Aideen and Colm's families, I want to offer you our sincerest condolences, not only on behalf of myself and my family, but on behalf of our entire community...*"

Gregory listened and watched the crowd, scrutinizing their faces and their reactions. Even if the population of Ballyfinny wasn't already over ninety per cent 'White Irish', he would still have predicted the killer to be of the same ethnicity as his victims, both of whom fell into that ethnic category. Unfortunately, knowing that didn't help very much, given the demographic.

"*To their killer, I want to tell you that we're onto you,*" Maggie was saying. "*We know why you killed Claire and Aideen, and we know you may be feeling overwhelmed by what you've done. Both myself and the Garda understand that you want to do the right thing. Come and turn yourself in, and put an end to the suffering...*"

In Gregory's experience, most killers knew when their behaviour was 'wrong'. With certain exceptions, all of his patients back at Southmoor knew and understood the difference between 'right' and 'wrong' but they chose to disregard that knowledge in the heat of the moment, or while they were planning to commit an offence. It was a matter of reminding them of this basic truth, so they would not feel compelled or driven to kill again.

So easy to talk about, but significantly harder to do.

Standing there on the side-lines, he was reminded of one of his earliest sessions with Cathy Jones. Back then, he'd believed what all clinicians like to believe, when they're new to a case. Namely, that the patient hadn't received the right treatment or the right therapy before. Fundamentally, it was an arrogant assumption to make, and he'd learned the error of his ways almost immediately.

"I don't know why I'm here, Doctor. They think I hurt my children but, I swear to you, I didn't…"

He could remember the earnest tone to her voice, the tears she'd shed, and had realised something very important.

No matter what he said, no matter what he did, Cathy Jones would never change, because she'd internalised the alternative fantasy world she'd created to justify her own actions. There were disorders he could name, syndromes he could ascribe, but it boiled down to something very simple.

She believed her own lies.

The crowd had begun to clap, and he raised his hands to join them.

The Ballyfinny Ladies' Circle met every Saturday afternoon at Molly's Tea Room, where they discussed the various happenings that week over endless rounds of Earl Grey and carrot cake. Some brought their knitting needles while others brought tiny, handbag-sized dogs that slept on their laps while their owners chewed the fat.

"I can hardly believe it," one of them was saying, between delicate bites. "I saw Aideen just yesterday morning, at the Post Office."

"And my Terence was over at O'Feeney's with Colm, just last night," another one whispered. "To think, the man died of his terrible, broken heart..."

"It was a heart attack, Mary," another one said, irritably. "Nobody dies of a 'broken heart."

"I declare they do," Mary replied, setting her cup back down on its saucer with a clatter of china. "There was never a man alive who loved his wife more than Colm loved Aideen. It's little wonder his heart couldn't stand the pain of losing her."

There was a flutter of hands against heaving bosoms, before the chatter started up again.

Molly listened to them from behind the counter as she rang up sales and moved between tables, collecting empty plates and dishing out fresh ones. As proprietor of the tea room since it opened back in the eighties, she knew every face in town and welcomed all of them, whether she enjoyed their company or not. The Ladies Circle were harmless enough on their own but, put them together and you had a simmering pot, ready to boil over.

"I tell you, it's the state of the world today. The *in-tur-net* and whatnot, driving people to murder each other..."

Molly heaved a long-suffering sigh and grabbed a notepad, before making her way to the table in the corner, beside the window.

"Hello, again!" she said, with a smile. "What'll it be?"

She took down the order, exchanged a few words of polite conversation and then busied herself putting scones on plates beside small ramekins of jam and cream. Behind her, the Ladies Circle talked of murder and of how they'd know who was responsible, as soon as they saw them. It would be as plain as the nose on their face.

Molly turned up the radio, partly to drown out their voices, but mostly to catch the local news report.

"*The Mayor of Ballyfinny gave a statement to the press, earlier today, in which she made a personal appeal to the Butcher to hand themselves in…*"

The person seated by the window smiled, and sipped their tea quietly.

CHAPTER 28

While Connor continued to oversee the forensic operation at the McArdle house, Alex accompanied Niall as he went about the business of re-interviewing the suspects who, by process of elimination, had found themselves at the top of his list of suspects. Unfortunately, first on that list was Tom Reilly, the school headmaster. Given all that Emma had confessed to him the night before, Gregory fervently wished he hadn't agreed to give her more time to build up the courage to tell her husband about her affair.

He glanced across at Niall's hard profile and wondered if she'd told him already.

Would it show?

Reilly lived in a comfortable, period property in the centre of town, not far from the school gates. There were two luxury cars parked on the driveway outside, and Niall let out a long whistle.

"Education pays," he said. "Or, his wife does. Kate Reilly has her own interior decorating company. Does over all the fancy properties hereabouts and is paid a pretty penny, so I'm told."

Gregory nodded towards the house.

"How come he made it onto your list?"

Niall ticked the reasons off his fingers.

"First, he knew Claire both personally and professionally, which means he would have known her routines. Second, it's less than half a mile between here and the Kelly house. The pathway runs right along past the school—and the McArdle house in the other direction. Third, he has a couple of pops for assault and disorderly behaviour, back when he was at university doing his teacher training. It's old, but you said to note down any past misdemeanours."

I did say that, Gregory thought.

"Fourth, the bloke has no alibi for the time Claire died. If you believe he was out jogging, you'll believe anything."

"It might be true," Gregory argued, and made a mental note to speak to Emma at the earliest opportunity. He could not continue to be party to a lie, no matter how well-intentioned.

"Aye, well. Let's see where he says he was last night," Niall said. "Perhaps he'll tell us he was out jogging then, too."

They made their way to the front door, which featured a stained-glass motif in the shape of a prancing horse.

Niall pulled an expressive face, which immediately transformed back into serious lines when the door swung open.

"Afternoon, Mrs Reilly. Is Tom at home?"

Kate was a very attractive woman, by many standards. Petite, slim and with a shining cap of blonde hair, she appeared in the doorway like a ray of sunshine, and had a smile to match.

"He is, yes. Is anything the matter?"

Niall shook his head.

"Not at all. We're just taking a turn around the town, checking some facts here and there. All strictly routine. Mind if we come in, darlin'?"

Kate led them inside and along a polished hallway to an enormous sunroom that looked as though it belonged on the centrefold of the latest *Homes and Gardens* magazine. There, they found Tom sprawled across an L-shaped sofa playing *Candy Crush* on his smartphone.

"Where are the kids?" she asked, with false brightness. "Aren't you supposed to be keeping an eye on them?"

"They're playing upstairs," he said, and his eyes flicked nervously between the two other men in the room. "Hello, inspector. And Doctor Gregory, isn't it? What brings you here?"

"We wondered if we could have a few minutes of your time," Niall said. "Sorry to interrupt you, on a Saturday an' all."

"No trouble," the other replied, and dragged himself upright. "Ah, why don't we sit in the snug? Can I get you a coffee or something?"

"We're fine, Tom—thanks all the same."

As they left the room, Gregory looked up to find Kate Reilly watching their progress, her eyes hooded and unreadable.

The 'snug' was an equally pristine feat of interior design, so much so they declined to sit on either of its immaculate, buttery leather sofas, in case they left a dent in the cushions. "Don't know why I bother coming in here," Tom grumbled. "Can't so much as fart, without her knowing about it."

"Ain't that the truth," Niall said. "Listen, Tom—I've a few questions I need to ask you, and I'm going to ask them under caution."

Reilly's smile faded.

"Under caution? What is this, Niall? Am I under arrest?"

"No, you're not under arrest, but we've two dead women on our hands, Tom. I've got a job to do."

Tom looked at Gregory, who was leaning against the wall nearest the door.

"Why's he here, then? I'm not a bloody lunatic—"

"Nobody's saying you are," Niall drawled. "Now, settle down, and tell me where you were last night, between the hours of five-thirty and ten."

Reilly's face cleared instantly.

"Oh, that's easy. I took Kate out for a meal, after work. Her Ma had the kids for the evening, so we had the night to ourselves."

Niall didn't bother to hide his surprise.

"Ah, d'you mind me asking which restaurant, and when?"

"Sure. We were over at O'Feeney's from around six o'clock until seven-thirty, then we walked over to The Olive Branch for dinner at quarter to eight."

"I see," Niall muttered. "And, I suppose there are people who could vouch for you?"

"Plenty, I'd say," Tom replied. "The restaurant was full, and the staff know us. I saw Colm McArdle in the pub before we left. Laughing away with his pals, poor soul. God rest him."

Niall asked a few more questions for good form, before turning to Claire's murder.

"The last time we spoke, you told me you'd been out for a long jog from around eight o'clock in the morning until past nine on the day Claire died. Do you have anything you'd like to add? Any details you might have missed and want to tell me now?"

Gregory watched Tom Reilly closely for his reaction, and was astounded by the man's ability to lie convincingly.

"It's like I told you, I was out jogging all morning."

"You weren't with Claire for any of that time?" Niall pressed, but Tom shook his head.

"It's like I said, things ended a long time ago between us."

Niall made a note, then asked him to sign it for the record.

"Thanks for the chat, we'll let ourselves out."

"Listen," the other man said, conspiratorially. "About Claire and me. You'll not say anything to Kate, will you?"

"If it's relevant to our investigation, we might have to,"

Niall warned him. "But I won't be calling her to spill your guts just for the fun of it, if that's what you mean."

They made for the door and Gregory took one last look at the school teacher before it closed behind them. He'd met all manner of pathological liars, during his time as a psychologist and—perhaps more importantly—as a citizen of the world, but few could match Reilly's finesse.

"Well, subject to speaking to the staff at the restaurant and the barman at O'Feeney's, it looks like Tom has a rock-solid alibi for last night," Niall said, once they were back in the car. "Makes me wonder if you weren't right, after all, Doc. Maybe he was out jogging, when Claire died."

"If it's the same person who killed both women, and I believe it is, then it looks as though he's out of the frame," Gregory agreed.

It was clear that Tom Reilly had chosen not to reveal his affair with Emma, which was understandable, since her husband was the man in charge of the town's most high-profile murder case for the past century. If Emma hadn't spoken to Niall about it herself, then Tom must have taken the decision to keep his own counsel to save her from embarrassment.

Just as Gregory had.

But then, head doctors such as he were good at keeping secrets.

CHAPTER 29

Father Sean Walsh was not at the abbey but was due back at around five o'clock. As that was only twenty minutes away, Niall and Gregory decided to wait, and were shown into the priest's study by one of the young seminarians who was training for the priesthood. As he left, Gregory wondered what kind of willpower it took for a nineteen-year-old lad to make the kind of life-changing decision to turn his back on the prospect of sex, or a family, but he supposed the answer would be that they were drawn to a 'higher calling'. When he thought of his own solitary existence and devotion to his patients and practice, he was forced to admit their two worlds were not so very different.

Except for the sex part.

"Ma will never forgive me for this," Niall said, interrupting his train of thought. "I've been back and forth, thinking about the right thing to do. He's a man of God, after all."

Gregory didn't think it an appropriate time to mention that men of God were still *men* and, therefore, more than capable of committing all manner of offences. As for Sean Walsh, he lived within striking distance of Claire and Aideen, had known them personally as their priest and, as they'd discovered, had grown up in the same miserable orphanage where Connor had spent the first six years of his life. Connor had been adopted, but Sean hadn't been so lucky. That meant there was plenty of scope for childhood trauma, especially growing up without a mother figure. Indeed, by all accounts, the only female role models in his early life had been strict, authoritarian and often cruel—the kind of women that could lead a young person to fantasise about what it might be like to have a 'real' mother who was loving and warm.

At least, before he killed them.

"Regardless of what he does for a living, your first duty is to protect the people of the town," Gregory said. "Father Walsh understands that, so I'm sure he'll be willing to cooperate, with no bad feelings."

Niall was pacing around the room. It was getting to that time of day again. The witching hour, when the sky outside started to turn dark and his thoughts turned to drink. Across the room, he spotted a crystal decanter filled with amber liquid and felt his throat run dry.

Gregory recognised the signs of withdrawal.

"You've been putting in some long days," he said, shifting his body so it blocked the decanter from view. "Long nights, too, I'll bet."

Niall nodded, and then sank into one of the chairs beside the faux-leather sofa Gregory remembered from the last time he'd been there.

"I'll be glad when it's over. We all will."

"Declan must be missing you."

Niall nodded, but a sadness passed over his face.

"To tell you the truth, I haven't been myself, lately. I probably haven't been the best father I could be, either."

Gregory took a seat beside him.

"We all have bad days," he said softly. "The key is to have a better day, tomorrow."

Niall rubbed a hand over his forehead.

"What if you can't see as far ahead as tomorrow?"

He glanced towards the door, then back at Gregory.

"I've been having these blackouts," he said, under his breath. "I'll wake up with no memory of how much time has passed, or where I've been."

Gregory showed no sign of surprise, and his ability to keep a straight face was part of the reason people found him so easy to talk to.

No judgment.

"How often have you been experiencing these blackouts?" Gregory asked.

He knew there were three main clinical reasons for a person to suffer a blackout: the first was owing to a 'syncope', or sudden lack of blood supply to the brain caused by poor blood pressure or existing heart problems; the second was epilepsy; and the third was known as a 'psychogenic blackout' resulting from extreme stress or anxiety.

There was also a fourth potential reason...

Alcohol abuse.

"It's happening two or three times a week," Niall admitted.

Before Gregory could quiz him any further, the door opened.

"Well," Father Walsh said. "This is a nice surprise."

The priest took his time removing the long over-cloak he wore on top of his cassock, then rubbed his hands together.

"Turning cold out there," he said. "Can I make you both some tea or coffee?"

"Only if you're making some for yourself, Father," Niall replied, and hated himself for hoping that the priest might have offered him a dram from the decanter.

"Simon tells me you've been waiting here a little while," he said, turning the kettle on to boil. "I'm sorry to keep you, but I had an appointment to visit the Kelly family today."

"How are they doing?" Niall asked.

"Well, now, I was pleased to find Liam in slightly better spirits than before. I don't mind telling you, I've been worried for him this past month, and for the child. Claire's death ripped a great hole in their lives. However, I'm pleased to say he's booked a trip to see the Cliffs of Moher, as a sort of pilgrimage to remind himself of a place where he and Claire were happy. He tells me it might help him to remember her in happier times."

"That's good news," Gregory said, and made no mention of it having been his suggestion.

"Indeed. Well, now. I think I can guess why you're here."

He handed them both mugs of steaming instant coffee.

"Why's that, Father?"

"You've looked at my history and the surrounding circumstances, and you'd like to know where I was when Claire Kelly and Aideen McArdle were killed. Is that right, my son?"

Niall felt all kinds of guilt, but he nodded.

"I'd rather ask you under caution, Father. It's been the same for everyone," he added swiftly.

"Don't berate yourself," the priest said. "I quite understand."

After the formalities were taken care of, Niall dived into his task. He was eager to get home, where he knew there was a bottle of single malt waiting for him.

"Would you mind telling us where you were last night, between the hours of six-thirty and ten?"

Walsh took a sip of his coffee.

"I was in here until about six, then I had an early dinner at home around six-thirty, following which I went for a walk along to the lough—oh, sometime around eight, I suppose. After that, I came home again, where I received a phone call from Maggie Byrne shortly after ten-thirty asking me to come along to see Colm, who'd suffered the worst kind of news. I believe you're aware of the rest."

Niall nodded.

"Was anybody with you, while you ate dinner or walked to the lough?"

Walsh took another sip of his coffee.

"No," he said. "They weren't. I'm afraid the same is true of the morning Claire Kelly died. On Saturday mornings, I use my time in quiet reflection, unless there's a special service or something of that kind."

"What about when Claire died? Where did you go— to reflect?"

"I remained here, in the quiet of my study," Father Walsh said.

Niall was silent for a moment, caught between his duty to his badge, and to the man who was the living embodiment of his faith.

"When you walked to the lough, did you take the woodland path?" Gregory asked, never having trembled in fear of God's wrath.

Walsh hesitated, then nodded.

"Yes, I did. I'm afraid I saw nobody suspicious as I passed by Aideen and Colm's home."

"I'm sure you could have handled any altercation, Father."

Both Niall and the priest turned to Gregory in surprise.

"I guess you had to be fairly streetwise, growing up at the orphanage," he elaborated. "Isn't that right?"

"Ah, I see."

Father Walsh set his cup down and linked his fingers over his stomach, in a relaxed gesture.

"You've read the news articles about what happened at St Hilda's and you imagine I suffered all kinds of abuse at the hands of the nuns, which served as a blueprint for deviant behaviour during adolescence and into adulthood, culminating in the murder of those poor people. Is that it?"

Niall looked supremely uncomfortable, but Gregory was unmoved. Many of his patients developed defence strategies that relied on what he thought of as 'British Reserve'— or, in this case, 'Irish Reserve.' Many people fell back on conventional manners so as to avoid an awkward social situation, such as the one they found themselves in now, which often allowed the wrong element to slip through the cracks.

"Did you?" Niall forced himself to ask, earning renewed respect from Alex in the process. "Did you suffer at the hands of the nuns, Father?"

When Sean closed his eyes, he could still feel the sting of their slaps, and the burn of their rods.

"Yes," he said quietly. "I did. As did many people, I'm sorry to say, in a scandal that brought shame on the Church I'm now proud to be a part of. I'm sure you've completed a thorough check of my background, so you'll know that, in my teenage years, I was a bit of a tearaway."

Niall merely nodded, and Gregory thought of the old juvenile reports he'd read about Sean Patrick Walsh, who'd spent much of his teens joyriding and engaging in petty theft.

"Until I found God, I had no direction in my life," Walsh explained. "I felt it had no meaning or purpose, until I stumbled into the small church in Kenmare, where somebody showed me kindness and another way of life."

"Do you know anything about your mother?" Gregory asked, and the priest nodded.

"I—yes, I do. The file they gave me when I left the orphanage listed my mother's first name and home town, and explained that she'd been a young woman of fifteen when she had me out of wedlock."

"May we see that record, Father?" Niall asked, but the priest shook his head.

"No," he said. "It would serve no purpose to reveal her name, now."

"Surely, Ireland's a big place—" Niall argued.

"It is, but my mother was born and still lives here in Ballyfinny," Walsh explained. "To reveal her name would be unfair to all concerned, especially as it has no bearing on the case you're investigating."

Gregory was struck by a sudden realisation.

"You know who she is, but she doesn't know you?"

The priest gave a small smile, and finished the last of his coffee.

"Of course," he murmured. "I've always known. Do you remember what I told you, Alex, about the sanctity of the confessional?"

Gregory nodded.

"It's the same reason why I will never willingly tell you the lady's name," he said. "If she was ever to find out that I was the child she lost, it would cause her great pain."

"And instead, you carry the burden of knowledge around with you," Gregory said. "That's an awfully heavy burden for any man, Sean. Don't you wish you could know your mother, properly?"

"I do," he replied. "More so than I might otherwise, for she tells me her secrets, her lies, her hopes and her fears each week, while I take comfort in the light of God."

CHAPTER 30

By the time they left the abbey, night had fallen. Cold wind rushed through the quiet streets and whipped up the fallen leaves that covered the ground in a patchwork of gold and brown. Gregory watched them and remembered when he was very young, kicking his way through the leaves in Hyde Park. He heard his own childish laughter as they'd risen up and fallen like confetti all around him.

"Alex?"

Niall called him over to the car, and he hurried to join the inspector on his final house call of the evening.

"About those blackouts," he said, once they were on the road. "Have you seen a doctor?"

Niall sighed.

"Look, forget I said anything," he muttered. "I don't need to see a doctor. I've just been tired, lately, and it's taking a toll, that's all."

"I really think you should have a check-up—"

"Look, thanks for the concern, but I'll see to it once this is all over and done with. Let's leave it at that."

Gregory fell silent, wondering what more he could do. Niall wasn't his patient—or even his friend.

They're all patients, aren't they?

Bill Douglas' words floated to the surface of his mind and he looked again at the careworn detective seated beside him.

"Where to, next?" he asked.

"Back to the hotel," Niall said, shortly. "I want to speak to my uncle and Padraig. Two more of my mother's favourite people, so that'll make a hat-trick for the day."

Gregory nodded.

"What did you make of Father Walsh's revelations?"

"Far as I can see, he's got no alibi for either murder," Niall replied. "And there's plenty of emotional baggage to play with, even for you."

Gregory sent him a mild look.

"It's never fun," he said. "But I agree that Father Walsh fits squarely within the profile. What about Padraig?"

"Paddy lost both of his parents a few years back," Niall explained. "He went a bit off the rails, with the drink and the drugs. My Ma helped him into a rehab program and he got himself clean again. Seamus gave him a chance working for the hotel. He seems back on track, now, but I can't discount that sort of history. Before she died, his mother was a hard woman."

"And he lives down near the hotel jetty," Gregory said. "That's less than half a mile away from Claire's house, but a little further away from Aideen."

"Aye, it's the wrong way around, for your profile—"

"It's just a guide," Gregory reminded him. "Don't stick to it too rigidly."

Niall nodded.

"Paddy's a quiet man, blends in and even works part-time as a postman," he said, pulling a face. "He knows these streets and pathways like the back of his hand, and everybody knows him."

"Has he ever been in a relationship?"

"Not that I remember," Niall replied.

"Any altercations or criminal misdemeanours?"

Niall nodded.

"When he was caught up in the drugs, Padraig dabbled in a bit of shoplifting here and there," he said. "He took a swing at a feller down at O'Feeney's, a couple of years back."

Gregory fell silent, considering the likelihood that the quiet, ruddy-faced man who worked at the hotel could be the killer they were looking for, and concluded that it was perfectly possible. He was a shy loner who'd missed having a mother figure in his life, and children like that often grew up to be teenagers looking for ways to escape. Drugs were one way of doing that, but building their own fantasy world was certainly another.

They found Padraig down by the boathouse, perched on the end of the small wooden jetty.

They might have missed him, were it not for the swirl of white smoke that rose up against the night sky as he smoked his way through one of his rollie cigarettes.

"Evenin' Paddy," Niall said, as their footsteps clattered across the wooden slats. "Mind if we join you?"

"Free country," he replied.

He'd draped a thick blanket over his shoulders and, beneath that, he wore his customary wax jacket. Neither Gregory nor Niall had intended to sit outside in the cold weather, and they were already beginning to shiver in response to the icy blast rolling in from the water.

"On second thought, any chance we could move this indoors?" Niall asked. "I'm freezin' m' bollocks off, out here."

Padraig let out a grunt, which might have passed for a laugh, and rose to his feet.

"This way."

They followed him back along the jetty towards the boathouse, and beyond that to a tiny cottage. The Land Rover was parked alongside, and Gregory asked whether it had been fixed.

"Engine's gone," Padraig replied. "I'll take it apart tomorrow."

Inside, the cottage was cosy. The front door led immediately into a narrow porch that reeked of dry mud and led directly into the living space, which also served as the kitchen and dining room, both of which were spotlessly clean.

Padraig kicked off his rubber boots and hung his coat on a single peg by the door, then indicated that they should sit in one of the three armchairs arranged in a triangular formation around a log-burning fireplace. Gregory wondered why there were three chairs, and Padraig must have read his mind, for he answered the unspoken question.

"Three's more'n enough," he said gruffly. "Any more's a crowd."

He moved to the kitchen area and pulled out a bottle of whiskey, about three-quarters full.

"Drink?" he asked them.

Niall stared at the bottle and felt the tug in his system, the yearning for a taste—

"Thanks, Paddy, but we're still 'on duty'," Gregory answered, deftly taking the decision out of his hands.

Niall felt a wash of anger rage through him, frightening in its intensity—then it was replaced by an even more shameful feeling of tearful desperation.

To hide it, he took a turn around the room.

"Like what you've done with the place," he joked, looking around the room at the spartan décor.

"I've no use for trinkets," Padraig replied. "All they do's sit around, gatherin' dust."

Gregory happened to agree with him.

"So, come to ask if I did it, have you?"

Padraig threw back a finger of whiskey and set the glass back on the counter.

"Thought you'd have come knockin' before now."

"We're asking a lot of people, Paddy—"

"You'd better ask your questions, then, and be on your way."

Niall nodded.

"Fair enough," he said, and recited the standard cautionary words. "Do you understand?"

"It's not the first time I've heard it said," Paddy replied. "Aye, I understand, right enough."

"Good. Then, can you tell me where you were last night, between the hours of five-thirty and ten?"

Gregory watched panic flit over the man's face, before it was masked.

"I was here, till after eight, then I took a wander over to O'Feeney's. Saw Colm McArdle in there."

"Anybody vouch for you?"

"Anybody who was in there, same time I was," came the surly response.

"Alright," Niall said. "You say you were here until eight. Can anybody confirm that?"

There was the briefest of hesitations, then Padraig shook his head and reached for the whiskey bottle again.

"Didn't see anyone on the path into town, neither."

"Which path do you normally take into town, Padraig? The one that runs through the hotel grounds past the tennis courts, or the road that runs over the bridge?"

He looked over at Gregory, and gave a slight shrug before downing his second finger.

"Depends whereabouts I'm going," came the cryptic reply.

Just then, the outer door opened without a warning knock, and Seamus Murphy let himself into the cottage.

"Paddy, I—oh, sorry! I didn't realise you had visitors. Hello Niall, Alex," he said. "I, ah, Paddy, the boiler on the second floor isn't working properly and a couple of the guests have complained. I wonder if you'd mind coming to have a look at it?"

"I'll be up in a minute," he said.

Seamus excused himself, with an embarrassed smile.

"Must be nice to have such a friendly boss," Gregory remarked. "Most people would just use the phone."

"We're a friendly bunch, for the most part, round here," Niall said.

"Evidently," Gregory muttered.

As the skies darkened outside, the red-headed woman pottered around the living room, scooping up toys from the floor before dumping them into a wicker basket in the corner with a teddy bear embroidered on the front. She hummed to herself, some old show tune she'd heard on the radio, while her mind wandered.

She worried for her child.

And she was right to; there was plenty to be concerned about. The long, quiet spells, the mood swings and tantrums—they were all out of the ordinary.

But what could she do?

From the shadows outside, they continued to watch her. She was a tall, slender woman with fine-boned hands and strong shoulders; strong enough to bear the burden of two people. She had a soft voice and pale skin that bruised as easily as a peach.

The woman threw the final toy into the basket—then paused, suddenly, and looked around the room.

Were there tears in her eyes?

There would be, soon enough.

CHAPTER 31

Sunday

The baby was crying again.

Alex heard it, louder than ever before, through the walls of the confessional box. He tried to get out, but there was no door and it was so dark. He ran his fingers over the wooden walls, desperately seeking a way out, the pads of his fingers beginning to tear as he clawed away at the darkness that seemed to be closing in, all around him.

"Help! Help me!"

"God is listening, my son."

He held himself very still as a whispering voice filled the small space. From nowhere, two candles ignited, one slightly larger than the other, illuminating the small space with their faint glow. Through a small, cross-hatched window he saw a shadowy figure with their face in profile.

"Who is it?" he cried out. *"Tell me who you are!"*

"*You know who I am,*" the voice replied. "*You've always known.*"

"*What do you want? Tell me what you want!*"

Suddenly, the figure turned and pressed its face against the window, pushing forward until its eyes bulged against the cross-hatched wood.

"*I want my rosary,*" Cathy hissed. "*Give me my rosary back.*"

Her tongue darted out, forked at the end, and became a snake, slithering through the gaps in the wood. It fell onto the floor at his feet and writhed around there while Alex pressed himself back against the wall, frantically seeking a doorway.

She laughed, and then turned to blow out the two small candles.

In the darkness, black as night, he screamed.

Gregory awakened to a loud, banging noise.

At first, he imagined it was the sound of his own fists as he fought to break through the wood of the confessional box. Then, when the banging grew more persistent, he realised it was coming from the door of his hotel room.

"I'm coming!" he called out, and heaved himself off the bed to find some pyjama bottoms.

He didn't own any, so he tugged on the trousers he'd worn the previous day and then hurried to answer the door.

Maggie stood on the other side of the doorway, dressed

in jogging pants and a matching hoodie in a fetching shade of pale pink. On her feet, she wore her ubiquitous brown boots and her grey hair stood out at all angles. The overall effect was something high-end stylists probably took hours to create.

"Thank the good Lord," she declared, and turned to her brother, who was hovering nearby. "Call off the cops, Seamus, our boy here's just had a nightmare, by the looks of things."

"Sounded like bloody blue murder," he said, peering first at Gregory's clammy face and then over his shoulder into the hotel room, as if to make sure an intruder wasn't lurking somewhere behind the brocade curtains.

"I'm sorry to wake everyone," Alex said. "Please apologise to the other guests—"

"Never mind about that," Maggie said, waving away the formality. "Besides, it'll probably boost the hotel ratings on *TripAdvisor* if people start to say the place is haunted."

Seamus visibly perked up.

"D'you think that's true?"

Maggie rolled her eyes.

"Aye, Seamus. Now, why don't you get off back to bed and start planning those ghost tours?"

When he headed off, Maggie looked Gregory up and down.

"At least you're decent," she said, and stepped inside the room. "A woman of my position and obvious attractions needs to protect her reputation, you know."

Gregory grinned and closed the door behind her.

"You shouldn't have come all the way over, just because I was having a nightmare," he said.

"Seamus didn't know what else to do. He couldn't get the door open, and it honestly sounded as though someone was in there murdering you."

"I'm sorry," he said again. "I left the telephone off the hook and I have a habit of leaving the key in the door when I lock it, so he probably couldn't use the same keyhole from the outside to open it."

The hotel was one of those rare breeds that hadn't resorted to key cards.

Maggie looked across at the bed, with the covers halfway on the floor and the pillows thrown across the room. A desk chair stood just to the left of the door, looking very much out of place, and she guessed it had recently been tucked beneath the door handle as an added layer of defence.

Against what, she didn't know.

"If behaviour mirrors personality, then I'd say you're a wee bit jumpy there, Alex."

Gregory huffed out a laugh, and walked over to the coffee machine. It was after four, and he knew there'd be no chance of getting any further sleep that night.

"Coffee?"

Maggie nodded, and automatically straightened the covers on his bed.

"Do they always haunt you?" she asked.

"The dead, or the living?" he replied.

"Either. Both."

He handed her one of the fancy glass coffee cups the hotel had provided.

"Either and both," he said, and clinked his cup against hers before downing an espresso in one gulp.

"It sounded like a bad one was chasing you tonight," she said, and took a seat on the sofa beside the window, so she could watch the dawn rising over the lough. "Want to talk about it?"

Alex was tempted.

It would be so easy to slide into conversation with this warm, understanding woman who could laugh at the darkest of moments.

"Your sons are lucky to have you," he said quietly. "It's that kind of generosity of spirit the killer covets. They're desperate for what you've just offered me; a tiny piece of your heart, which is big enough to share. Be careful, Maggie. There are people out there who see it—and want to make sure nobody else ever does."

She heard the warning but, beneath that, she heard pain.

Saying nothing, she got up and walked around to where he stood beside the window, and put her arms around him, where they stayed for long minutes until the fight drained out of him.

———

Later, when the sun had risen and Maggie had returned to her own home, Alex went for a long swim in the hotel pool. It helped to shake off any remaining disquiet following what had, admittedly, been one of the worst nightmares he'd experienced in a while—and to focus his mind on what was really important.

Finding the killer's next target.

The interviews Niall had conducted the previous day had only served to throw up more possibilities. Every one of them, with the exception of Tom Reilly, had the means, opportunity and moreover the unique personality type to kill. Each had unresolved issues with a mother figure and had suffered childhood trauma of some form or another.

None of that took into account the trustworthiness of the Garda detectives themselves. Despite asking more than once, Niall and Connor had failed to provide him with a statement giving their whereabouts at the time of both murders. Niall admitted to being at home alone on Saturdays, thereby giving him ample opportunity to walk to the Kelly house. That still left Friday night, when Aideen died. Connor was in even worse shape, having told him he was manning the Garda station alone on the Saturday morning when Claire died, but giving no information at all about his whereabouts on the Friday night, either.

Gregory quickened his kick, slicing through the water as he considered his next move. Eggs would be broken, he thought, and remembered Maggie's face when she'd told him about Niall and Connor. He only hoped the damage could be repaired, before all was said and done.

CHAPTER 32

By the time Gregory made his way into Ballyfinny, the wind had changed.

In the far distance, dark clouds were gathering and, though it remained bright over the lough, it was as though the animals sensed that a storm was brewing. There was no sound of birdsong in the trees, nor the rustle of woodland mammals scavenging in the brush.

All was silent and still.

The wind had changed direction at the Garda station, too.

Many of the support staff and guards had taken themselves off to Sunday Mass, but Connor, Niall and a few other key members of staff remained to deal with a new maelstrom that now threatened their investigation. It came in the form of Superintendent Carole Donoghue, whom Gregory recognised as the tall, blonde woman who'd attended the police briefing at the hotel the day before. She was Niall's direct superior at Divisional Headquarters in Castlebar and had been given orders to remove Niall, Connor and Gregory from the case.

"Ma'am—with respect—why are you doing this? We've been working around the clock to find this arsehole," Connor argued.

"I'm under orders from Garda Headquarters," she said, flatly. "They've received complaints and allegations of police bias, owing to your familial relationship, not to mention your ties to the Mayor. They've also expressed concerns about the level of credence being given to the profile produced by Doctor Gregory."

All three men spoke at once, and she held up her hands.

"This isn't up for debate," she said. "They didn't like the headlines after the press conference, and, frankly, neither did I."

"That's what this is really about," Niall said, with obvious disgust. "They're worried about their precious politics, again. Can't have anybody making the Chief Constable look bad, can we?"

"That's enough," Donoghue said. "I've had the brass buzzing in my ear all morning and I've had it up to here."

She flattened her palm and gestured to a height above her own head.

"Niall, I want you back at Castlebar and at your desk by lunchtime," she ordered. "Connor? You can stay on here, but strictly as family liaison since the locals know you. And…"

She side-stepped the two detectives and walked over to where Gregory was standing, just inside the doorway, awaiting his turn at the executioner's block.

"Doctor Gregory, I want to thank you for the work you've done for our department," she said, sincerely. "Whilst I'm under orders to take over the investigation and to bring our working relationship with you as a consultant to an end, I'd like to say that I found your discussion highly informative at the briefing yesterday. I may be under orders, but I don't necessarily agree with them. I happen to believe that profilers and the police can work very well together, and often do."

He read between the lines.

"Thank you," he said. "And, of course, I fully understand your position. Although I'm quite happy to relinquish any formal relationship the Garda has with me, I hope you won't mind if I stay on for a few days, here in Ballyfinny. I'm due some holiday time."

She cocked her head to one side.

"Doctor, you wouldn't be planning to hang around the town hoping you might be able to work with us in an informal capacity, and risking further embarrassment to the pencil pushers in Dublin, now would you?"

"Wouldn't dream of it," he said. "But, if I did, I'd also tell you that the person you're looking for won't wait as long as they did last time. They're more skilled, more confident and, on some level, more aware that they can't continue their spree indefinitely. They're running out of time—and so are we."

Donoghue nodded, and spoke in an undertone.

"I'll have officers patrolling twenty-four hours a day, for the next seven days," she said. "Are there any in particular on your list of suspects that you feel we should keep under surveillance?"

Gregory let out a long breath.

"Several are near-perfect fits for the profile I created, and which I still stand by," he replied. "But I think you should keep an extra close eye on the church, and in the meantime, seek a search warrant to seize copies of Father Walsh's personal papers. In there, it lists the name of the mother who gave him up as a baby, and she's still living here in Ballyfinny. She could be an intended target."

Donoghue's eyes darkened.

"Failing that, look at recent traumas to narrow the pool," he murmured. "Deaths, marriages, even births. Look for where a relationship has broken down or they've been rejected in some other way. It's in there, somewhere."

Donoghue held out a hand, which he shook.

"I'll be in touch," she said.

CHAPTER 33

A brief phone call to the Hospital Director at Southmoor had bought Gregory three extra days in Ballyfinny, after which he needed to return to his duties and his patients back in England. It was frustrating to know that political intrigues and public relations held more sway with senior Garda officials than fact-based research—or hundreds of man-hours spent on the ground getting to know a community, as Niall and Connor had done—but he knew that, in matters of public perception, it was not only about doing the right thing; it was about being *seen* to do the right thing. For that reason, it was the right move to pull Niall and Connor Byrne off the case and to allow them to be eliminated from the list of potential suspects—or not, as the case may be.

On his way back to the hotel, Gregory put another call through, this time to Bill Douglas.

"Two conversations in one week? It must be my birthday," Douglas quipped.

"Is it a bad time?"

"It's a perfect time," Douglas replied. "One of my tutorials was cancelled, so I'm unexpectedly free. What's up?"

"An order came from above to shake up the investigation," Gregory told him. "I don't disagree with it, since the basis of the case has changed fundamentally over the past week or so. In the beginning, when the Garda believed they were looking for an outsider, it was acceptable to have a local man and his brother running the show."

"But now they know it's someone local, they need an outside task force," Douglas concluded. "I wonder who had a word in their ear."

"I spoke to the superintendent in Castlebar first thing this morning," Gregory admitted. "Neither of the Byrne brothers is being open about their movements and they both fit the profile. It was the right thing to do and will make for a more transparent investigation, going forwards."

There was a second's pause, and then Douglas barked out a laugh.

"You're a cool one," he said. "What'll they say, when they find out you went over their heads?"

"Niall and Connor won't thank me," Gregory admitted. "Neither will their mother. But, if the Garda *don't* find who's responsible and the killings just stop, as they sometimes do, they'll forever have the Sword of Damocles over their heads. People in the community will always wonder, just as they will about the priest and every other person who fits the profile. This way, at least they can be investigated and eliminated. I'm trying to help them to help themselves."

He didn't add that, with Niall Byrne suffering blackouts, he had separate concerns about that man's welfare and overall capacity to do the job. Besides, he had a wife and child to think of—both of whom might be at risk themselves.

Douglas leaned back in his desk chair, which overlooked the beautiful campus quadrangle at Hawking College, Cambridge.

"All the same, they won't like it."

"They don't have to."

Douglas marvelled at his friend's ability to shut out the noise of social convention, in order to do what he felt was right. It wouldn't win him any friends, but it might stop a killer. To Alex Gregory, one was vastly more important than the other.

"Are the Garda keeping you on, to consult?" Douglas asked.

"Not formally," he replied. "I've told the new superintendent that I'll be staying on for a couple more days, if she needs me."

As Gregory entered the pine forest, the line began to crackle.

"Are you any closer to finding the offender?" Douglas asked.

"I understand them, and why they're driven to kill. There's still nothing in the way of useful DNA to help us, so it's a case of closing the net by looking at other variables. We're much closer than we were a few days ago, unfortunately, thanks to them having killed again."

It was a sad truth that, the more victims he was able to study, the more data they were able to gather, and the closer they came to finding the perpetrator. But that wasn't much comfort to the families of those who had been lost.

"Whatever happened with that woman—Emma, was it?"

"Nothing you need worry about," Gregory replied. "It turns out, she had an affair with one of the people on the suspect list, thereby giving him an alibi for the first murder of Claire Kelly. It's another reason for Niall to take a step back; as her husband as well as the investigating officer, he can't be impartial. It's already prevented either Emma or this other man coming forward with the truth."

"Complicated," Bill muttered. "Are you going to tell the Garda, or did Emma tell you this information in the context of a clinical discussion?"

Gregory paused to give the question due consideration.

"No, I think she was speaking to me as a friend, and as a profiler. She wanted me to know that this man Tom Reilly wasn't a killer, but didn't want to have to tell her husband about the affair. If Niall wasn't a detective, she wouldn't have needed to make the choice."

"But he is, so she does. And there's only one right choice."

"That's exactly what I told her," Gregory said. "I agreed to give her a couple of days to come out with it. Now that Niall's no longer on the case, there should be nothing to prevent her coming forward with the information to the new superintendent."

"Clever," Bill approved. "You found a way to protect her. I wonder why?"

Gregory thought of the child, Declan, and his father.

And, yes, he thought of Emma.

He opened his mouth to say something else, but found the telephone signal had cut out, taking his friend with it. He slipped the phone back into his pocket and, without Bill's comforting voice at his ear, was suddenly very aware of how alone he was.

He stopped for a moment and looked around him, at the various pathways diverging in the middle of the pine-scented wood, and knew that only one would be the right one.

Maggie Byrne was peeling potatoes for a roast dinner when a knock came at her door.

Wiping her hands on the edge of a tea towel, she thought about not answering it; afraid it would be more reporters clamouring for a story. Aideen McArdle was lying on a cold slab down at the mortuary in Galway Hospital next to her husband—side by side, even in death. But it was her family that bore the brunt of press speculation and intrusion, and she had a word or two to say about that.

When she threw open the front door, the words died on her lips.

"Oh, it's only you. For a minute, I thought it was one of that lot from the *Dublin Enquirer*," she muttered. "Come in, Alex."

Gregory wiped his feet and stepped inside, where he soon realised they were not alone.

"Hi!"

Declan appeared at the bottom of the stairs, carrying a small tub of Lego.

"Want to build something?" he asked, and Gregory realised that he did.

He wanted to sit and build towers and planes. He wanted to be young again and to see the world through a prism of unfettered optimism, where he no longer worried about what people had seen, what they had done, or what lay behind their eyes.

He wanted to build Lego houses.

But there were things he needed to say to Maggie; things that couldn't wait.

"I'll come and build something with you later, if I'm able," he said, and watched the boy trot into the living room with his plastic box.

"Is Emma here too?" he asked.

"She's running an errand for me," Maggie said. "Do you need to talk to her?"

"Later," he said. "It's you I've come to see."

There was a catch to his voice that she didn't like, but she led him into the kitchen, where she shook out a couple of tea bags.

"This sounds serious," she said. "What's happened, now? Has there been another one?"

Alex rested his hands on the back of one of the kitchen chairs.

"No, there hasn't been another one that I know of," he said, and then came to the point. "Maggie, you won't like what I'm about to tell you, and I'm prepared for that. But I want you to know two things before I say what I need to say. The first is that I acted with your best interests at heart, as well as those of your family."

She dropped the tea bags into two bone china mugs, then turned to look at him. But he saw no anger there, only concern.

That made things even harder.

"Go on," she said. "You're worrying me, Alex."

"The second thing is that it's been a privilege to get to know you. Not only did you entrust me to help your community at a vulnerable time, you made me feel like one of that community and you invited me into your home. I'm grateful to you for that, and I won't forget it."

"Alex, for God's sake, what's the matter?"

"Superintendent Donoghue has taken Niall and Connor off the investigation," he began.

"*What*? Why?"

She was incredulous.

"Because I suggested it was the right thing to do, when I rang her early this morning."

Gregory watched the shock and dismay cross her face, but he held firm.

"Why would you do such a thing?"

"Because it was in their best interests, and those of the town, but Niall wouldn't have suggested it himself."

"How'd you figure that one out?" she asked, and he saw that she was the Mayor again, despite her casual clothes and the homely setting. By the regal look in her eye, she could have been standing at the steps of Buckingham Palace.

"Niall and Connor won't divulge their whereabouts last night," he said. "The press is here in double digits, and they're asking a hell of a lot of questions. Someone, somewhere, is going to start asking about the police and, when they do, questions will be raised about why nobody had demanded they provide a statement or at least eliminate themselves from the enquiry."

"Has—has anyone complained?" she asked.

Gregory nodded.

"Donoghue told me they'd had a couple of separate complaints, so it's likely they would have removed Niall or Connor from the investigation, anyway. But I'm not trying to detract from what happened. I wanted to tell you this, and to explain why I made the recommendation."

"I think I'm beginning to understand," she said, icily.

He shook his head.

"In many serial killer cases like these, where the offender is extremely careful and they leave little or no forensic trace, it's unlikely that the police team will apprehend them. That's basic fact," he said. "Sometimes, the killings will stop for a period of time and nobody can work out why. It may be that the killer's had a change of plan or life circumstance, has moved, or something else has interfered. If that were to happen here, I don't want either Niall or Connor to be wrongly suspected of involvement."

"They wouldn't be. Not so long as—"

"So long as their Mama can watch over them?" he asked softly. "Maggie, you know that's what people would start to wonder, just as they'd wonder about Sean Walsh, Padraig or any number of others who don't have an alibi and who fit the bill."

Maggie turned away.

"Say that's true," she said eventually. "There's no need to have them taken off the case."

"You mean to tell me, not one person has raised the issue with you?" Gregory asked. "Nobody's questioned the fact that Niall's your boy, and Connor, too?"

Maggie's lips trembled. Of course, people had questioned it; as the death toll continued to rise, so too did people's suspicions.

"When people thought the killer was an outsider, there was no problem," Gregory said. "But it's different now. They know it's one of their own, and Niall and Connor are part of that. In the interests of due process, they have to be eliminated."

She knew it was true, Maggie thought. And yet…

"I've seen what happens in cases like these," Gregory said, willing her to listen. "When the media get involved and the public get to know about the tragedy, they demand something new every day. They want to know progress is happening and, if it isn't happening quickly enough, or in the direction they want, the tide turns. Soon enough the people who'd once been supportive turn out to be the greatest critics. They look for police failings, and then they hang people out to dry."

Maggie leaned back and folded her arms.

"That's what happened to you, three years ago," she said. "It doesn't mean the same thing would happen to Niall or Connor. They're not strangers here, they're—"

She stopped abruptly.

Part of the fabric, she'd been about to say. The same words used to describe a killer who was running amok.

"Nobody is above suspicion, Maggie. Not even you. Do you think we didn't consider you, as a credible suspect? The difference is, you have an alibi for the Friday nights and Saturday mornings in question."

Her mouth gaped open, and he almost laughed.

"I—well, there's a thing," she said, for once not finding the words to describe the unique emotion that came with knowing her own children had considered her aptitude for murder. "I look after Declan most Friday nights, and Saturday mornings, to give Niall and Emma a chance to be alone and work on their relationship."

He nodded.

"I know, and it's a kind thing to do. The only problem is, Niall doesn't always spend those Friday nights at home with Emma. She doesn't know where he goes, and he won't tell us."

Maggie sighed, and shook her head.

"Always was a law unto himself."

CHAPTER 34

It took more time and some persuasion, but, eventually, Maggie understood Gregory's reasons for suggesting a change of Garda personnel. Part of her even admired him for doing it and, if it meant that her sons would be removed from the list of suspects who could have committed murder, that was all to the good. But, just as Gregory was eventually allowed to build a bridge—albeit from Lego bricks—things became much worse.

Emma hurried inside the cottage and called out to her mother-in-law.

"Maggie!"

"What is it, love?" she asked, stepping back into the hallway. "What's the matter?"

"I just had a call from Niall. He says Donoghue had a tip-off from the press and she's taking it seriously. *The Tribune* are saying they received an anonymous call from one of the locals here in Ballyfinny, claiming they saw Connor bury a plastic bag down by his boat hut—on the Saturday morning after Claire Kelly died. Maggie, they're saying he looked agitated, and they think it could be suspicious."

"I thought he was manning the station that Saturday morning," Gregory said, closing the living room door so Declan wouldn't overhear.

Emma swept her eyes over his face, and it was as though she'd touched him.

Gregory looked away, his fist curving around the Lego brick he held in his hand.

"He *was* at the station," Maggie said, and failed to pick up on any nuance while her mind was occupied elsewhere. "If my boy said he was at the station, then that's where he was."

"Where's Connor now?" Gregory asked.

"Niall says Connor's taken the superintendent down to his boat hut," Emma replied. "He's adamant they'll find nothing there, but Niall wants us to call a solicitor, anyway."

"If Connor's certain he has nothing to hide, why do we need the solicitor?" Maggie asked, a bit desperately. "He'll show this woman his hut and that'll be the end of it."

"I think we should get down there, Maggie," Gregory said. "You might be his mother, but you're also the mayor of the town. It won't hurt to be present, to make sure everything's done by the book."

That put a different complexion on things, and she grabbed her handbag and keys, ready to hurry down to the lough. There was a moment when she might have asked Gregory not to come with her, but then it passed, and she jerked her head towards the door.

"You coming or not?"

Gregory smiled, and handed the Lego brick to Emma as he rushed out of the house.

"Tell Declan I said 'goodbye'," he said. "And that I hope he builds some good, strong bridges. You never know when you might need them."

———————

Sergeant Connor Byrne owned a small fishing hut on the banks of the lough, a half-mile or so away from the Kelly house, as the crow flies. It was accessible from the lough trail, which was a pathway that ran the entire circumference of the water and was met by a number of smaller pathways leading down, used by locals to access their boats. The hut itself was the kind of bijou affair that city folk paid a lot of money to visit for the weekend, being both small and quaint, with outstanding views of the lough and blue-grey hills beyond. It had been built near the water's edge, just off the main trail, so dog-walkers and fellow fishing enthusiasts, as well as the occasional stray tourist, walked past on a fairly regular basis. But now, a team of Garda officers and a small forensic unit led by Superintendent Donoghue blocked the pathway as they prepared to conduct a search of what had once been Connor's retreat, but would be no more from that day forward.

Gregory arrived with Maggie soon after the search began, following a brisk walk down the woodland pathway from the road. It pained his mother to see Connor flanked by Donoghue and another sergeant drafted in from Castlebar, but she was encouraged to find Niall standing a short distance away, behind the police cordon but close enough to keep an eye on proceedings.

"Niall—thank God, you're here," she said, and pulled him in for a hard hug. "Tell me what on Earth's going on. How's Connor?"

"Putting a brave face on it, far as I can tell," her son replied. "It was his idea to do the search."

"What's this madness I hear, about him stashing away a plastic bag?" she asked. "It sounds crazy."

"No doubt, it is," he agreed. "But, with things being the way they are, Donoghue can't leave any stone unturned. Connor understands that, and he wants to clear his name. Neither of us want there to be any suggestion of special treatment because we happen to be Garda men."

Maggie glanced towards Alex, who nodded.

"I'm glad you feel that way," he said. "Because I need to tell you that I was partly responsible for you and Connor being dropped from the investigation. As the offender is a local person, and so are you, the situation opened itself up to allegations of bias that are best avoided. You have a reputation for being a man of integrity, as does your brother, and I acted in the way I felt would best ensure your reputation remains intact."

Niall fingered the paperclip he kept in his trouser pocket while he considered whether to punch Gregory in his interfering face.

"You think you know best, eh?" he said. "You think you can go over my head and take away my chance to make the collar, is that it?"

"No—"

"You didn't think you should talk to me first?" he continued, taking a step forward. "Or Connor?"

Gregory raised an eyebrow and held his ground.

"I did talk to you," he reminded him. "Several times, where I asked you to tell me your whereabouts on Friday nights, and when you promised to supply me with formal statements to that effect. They never arrived. If you have personal matters to see to, it's only right that you stand aside."

"Niall, listen to what the man has to say," Maggie urged, when he would have erupted.

"I don't think so, Ma. I reckon I was right all along. Our Doctor Gregory's nothin' but a fame-seeker, out to make a name for himself off the backs of people like me."

With that, he turned and began to walk away, only to pause at the sound of a commotion beside the hut. One of the forensic team who'd been excavating a shallow, recently dug-out hole, set aside their shovel and pulled a black plastic bag from the ground.

"Jesus," Niall whispered. "It can't be."

When they held up a woman's dress, stained a dark, brownish-red, Maggie began to weep softly.

The nearest Garda station with holding cells and an interview suite was Divisional Headquarters at Castlebar. While Niall accompanied Connor and arranged for a solicitor, Alex and Maggie followed shortly afterwards and made the forty-minute journey to the larger town, north of the lough.

"Storm's coming in," Maggie said. "It'll be with us before nightfall."

Ominous grey clouds loomed overhead, and the wind blew a steady gale, buffeting the edges of the car as they followed the narrow road around the water. The Weather Office had issued a 'yellow' warning advising people to avoid travel wherever possible, but there was no question of Maggie staying at home while her son languished in a cell.

There was a distant rumble, followed by the clap of lightning as they rounded the headland. "Four or five miles away," she estimated, and gripped the wheel a little tighter. "We'll want to get back on the road by four or five at the latest, if we want to miss the worst of it. The lower sections of this road are prone to flooding."

Gregory was happy to let her prattle on about the weather—it helped her to come to terms with the shock of Connor's arrest, while he thought about the killer profile. On many levels, there was a solid match in Connor Byrne. However, there remained a niggling doubt in his mind that rested upon one important detail integral to the killer's motivation: his desire for a mother figure. Claire Kelly and Aideen McArdle's killer coveted and punished at the same time. They used proxies to enact their fairy tale fantasy, while building up to removing the real, living person they felt had fallen so far short of the mark, or who may never have existed at all.

As far as he could tell, Connor and Niall Byrne had no need to look elsewhere for the fairy tale, because they had it already—and her name was Maggie. However, it was also true that perception came down to the individual. It was not so much a question of how the rest of the world perceived Maggie Byrne; it was how Connor and Niall perceived her that counted.

Gregory stole a glance at the woman driving the car, at the lines of worry pinching her skin, and considered how her children might think of her.

Authoritarian, maybe, but not domineering.

Loving, but not cloying or suffocating in her affection.

Supportive, but not dictatorial.

If Connor had ever felt lacking in a mother's affection, or if he had ever harboured a desire to punish, those dark emotions would more likely have been directed towards the nuns of St. Hilda's Orphanage and not at the woman who raced up hill and down dale through a gathering storm to help him.

But, if that was true, the question became: how had a bag full of bloodied women's clothing come to be found buried at the side of his hut?

Gregory meant to find out.

CHAPTER 35

Gregory barely noticed the streets and houses of Castlebar, so intent was he on trying to make sense of the most recent turn of events. He had a general impression of a town several times larger than Ballyfinny, with rail links to Dublin and other major towns across the country, and he spotted a couple of college campuses as they passed. However, as they met with traffic crossing one of the town's bridges on their way to the Garda station, he glanced outside and found his attention captivated immediately by the sight of a misty-blue mountain rising up in the far distance.

"That's Croagh Patrick," Maggie told him, and he heard the tiredness in her voice. "Folk around here call it 'the Reek'. A load of pilgrims climb it every year, on Reek Sunday, which is the last Sunday in July."

"Croagh Patrick," Gregory repeated. "Is that to do with Saint Patrick?"

Maggie nodded, and edged the car forward.

"Legend has it, Saint Patrick fasted and prayed on the summit of the Reek for forty days. There's a tiny chapel at the top and Patrick's Causeway, too, where folk can walk from Ballintubber Abbey to the Reek, if they've a mind to."

Gregory was reminded again of his detective friend in the North of England, whose beat included the island of Lindisfarne, which was a regular route for pilgrims who crossed the sandy causeway of that tidal island. He'd never felt any particular urge to go on a pilgrimage, but when he looked up at the purple-blue mountain with its arrow-headed tip, he felt strangely drawn to the idea.

Perhaps he would, one of these days.

The traffic moved on, and soon they were pulling into the visitor's car park at the Castlebar Garda Station, which served as the divisional headquarters for the Garda in that county. Its design was much more in line with what Gregory was accustomed to, consisting of a squat, pebble-dashed structure built sometime in the nineties during what appeared to have been a severe lull in architectural history.

Maggie caught his arm before they stepped inside.

"Alex, what if the unthinkable is true?" she asked, very softly. "What if everything I believed is wrong and Connor did these dreadful things? What do I do then? How do I face him, or the families—"

Gregory sensed a note of rising panic, and slipped a gentle arm around her shoulders.

"Nothing is certain, yet," he said. "Hear what Connor has to say, before coming to any conclusions."

She sniffed a little, holding back tears through strength of personality alone.

"You're right," she said, but her eyes were bleak. "But I keep thinking of the dog we had. That little dog…"

He held her close and they walked into the Garda station together.

As soon as they entered, Niall collected his mother and took her off to speak to their family solicitor and, afterwards, to see Connor. Meanwhile, Gregory went in search of Superintendent Donoghue and was told to wait in a small meeting room on the ground floor which smelled strongly of pot-pourri and stale sweat.

After twenty minutes, Donoghue entered the room with two cups of milky tea, laced liberally with sugar.

"I wasn't sure how you liked it, so I made it the same as mine."

"Thanks," he said, and took a polite sip of liquid glucose. "And thank you for agreeing to see me. I realise you must be very busy."

Carole smiled broadly, clearly very pleased at the turn of events.

"All we needed was a break," she said. "And I must thank you, Doctor. It was good instinct, and good sense on your part to suggest taking Connor and Niall off the case. Neither have full alibis and, as you rightly say, we need to consider all the residents of the town, not just those who don't happen to wear uniform."

She paused.

"As for Connor, even though he's a perfect fit for the profile, it's come as a shock to all of us here. We might investigate our own because we're professionals, but we still expect them to uphold the law. It's very disappointing. When I think of all the dinners and Christmas parties we went to…Anyway, I hope he'll do the right thing, when the time comes."

Gregory took another gulp of tea, and worried that he might be getting a taste for it.

"I think I need to clarify a couple of things, superintendent," he said. "When I said that everyone should be treated fairly and equally, including members of the Garda, that includes considering all material and circumstantial evidence—the profile I provided is not intended to act as a substitute for good police work."

Carole's face fell.

"Before we start talking unequivocally, let's remember that Connor Byrne is innocent until proven guilty. If material evidence pertaining to the murders has been found, I presume it's going to be fully analysed for DNA and compared with Connor's, as well as any of the other samples found at either of the crime scenes?"

"I—of course, yes," she muttered. "I thought you'd be happy that we've brought someone in. The NBCI are ecstatic…"

"I'll be happy if it's the right person," he shot back. "As it is, I can't be anywhere near sure that Connor is the person you're looking for, and I disagree that he's a perfect fit for the profile."

"Why?" she asked, and felt her buoyant mood begin to fade.

"For one thing, the act of keeping or burying a murder victim's clothes is not in keeping with the personality and behavioural traits of this kind of killer," he said. "Remember, they don't like ultra-violence. They're organised, not disorganised, and have a clear methodology that hasn't varied so far. That's because their purpose is to use their intended victim as a substitute, a kind of doll, that they can pose in whatever position they like. The theatrical staging is what gives the most insight: they're reimagining classic, childhood experiences. Once the experience is over, it's probably over, and they're seeking the next rush, the next opportunity to live out a fantasy they might not have experienced in their real childhood."

"Connor Byrne had a terrible start in life," she argued. "All of that is still consistent with a man who would have liked those 'normal' childhood tropes."

"But he had them, when Maggie came along," Gregory pointed out. "There's no need of a proxy, if you have somebody there filling in all those gaps, every day, for the rest of your life."

Donoghue acknowledged that was equally true.

"But coming back to the clothes you found today," Gregory leaned forward to reinforce the point. "In my experience, these kinds of killer don't tend to keep trophies. It's messy, it's dangerous, and it's unlikely that they're gleaning sexual gratification from any of this. It's a different kind of high they're looking for. The only reason they might have taken the clothing is most likely to destroy it elsewhere, or because it was contaminated with their DNA. Don't forget, they cleaned both crime scenes very thoroughly and, as far as I'm aware, you didn't find any cleaning rags, either. They're careful, and burying a bag of soiled clothing in a shallow grave beside your own fishing hut where any Labrador could dig it up isn't careful, it's downright sloppy."

Donoghue let out a long, pent-up breath of frustration.

"I have to follow the chain of evidence," she said, after a moment. "I have to follow up the tip-off we received, and not just because it's a new lead. It came via the press, and my commanding officer likes to keep them on side. I can't just ignore it."

Gregory said nothing at first, then he set his cup back on the table and made one final point for her to consider.

"I know you have to follow through," he acknowledged. "And I want you to, because that's the proper process. All I'm asking you to do is keep an open mind, and not write Connor off, just yet. There's a chance those clothes were planted by somebody else, particularly somebody who's aware of his background. The tip-off to the press was anonymous, wasn't it?"

She nodded.

"We haven't traced the source," she said.

"Right. And I'll bet you only found one set of clothes in that bag—Claire Kelly's, but not Aideen's?"

Donoghue was surprised.

"How did you know that?"

"I know, because experience has taught me that killers, especially organised ones, learn from their mistakes. With Claire Kelly, they weren't prepared for so much blood. It sounds silly, considering they planned to kill her, but the first time is always a shock. They probably made a mess with the dress, whereas in Aideen's case, they already knew what to expect. They made her undress first, killed her in the downstairs shower room, then simply put the old dress back on her, afterwards. Am I right?"

Carole smiled appreciatively.

"You're absolutely right," she said. "But all that doesn't remove the possibility that it might have been Connor who was taken by surprise, and Connor who was forced to take Claire Kelly's clothing away with him."

He had to admit, that was true.

It was a stalemate.

CHAPTER 36

Leaving Maggie in the capable hands of her son, Gregory went off in search of a taxi. However, every rank from the station to the shopping centre was empty, and he realised he'd forgotten something the mayor had told him the very first time he'd landed at Knock Airport. The young people of the county liked to travel to Galway on weekends to enjoy its bright lights, and they booked out most of the county's fleet in advance. Even without that complication, they were hardly overrun by taxi firms willing to travel long distances over dangerous roads. With the forecast looking increasingly bleak outside and the air temperature dropping swiftly, Alex decided there was little else to do but put a call through to the Ballyfinny Castle Hotel, where Seamus took pity on him and instructed Padraig to collect him in one of the hotel cars.

He expected to wait at least forty minutes in the foyer of the Castlebar Garda Station, but Padraig pulled up a mere twenty-five minutes later, leaving him to question how the man had managed to shave off a full fifteen minutes of a winding cross-country drive without happening to own a car that could fly.

"Thanks for coming all this way," he said, buckling himself in. "Guess you know all these roads like the back of your hand."

"Y' could say that."

"Weather forecast isn't looking good."

"Can't say I bother looking, anymore."

"Been busy, up at the hotel?" Alex asked, moving on to the second chapter of *Small Talk for Awkward Social Occasions*.

"Fair," the other man replied.

For reasons unknown, that made Gregory laugh. Perhaps it was the man's irreverence, or his flagrant disregard for social conventions. Either way, Padraig was one of a kind.

"I'm liable to go deaf, if you keep talkin' my ear off like that."

Padraig rubbed the side of his nose, to hide a smile.

"Them who're the quietest have the loudest minds, so they say," Padraig replied, and flung them both to the left as he flew over a roundabout.

"Must be a proper Riverdance concert going on in your head."

They fell into a contented silence, each man feeling satisfied he'd held up his own end. They didn't speak again until Padraig was halfway around the lough road that would lead them back to the hotel.

"Came as a surprise, Connor being arrested."

Once Gregory had overcome his own surprise at the conversation starter, he agreed.

"It's a blow to Maggie."

Padraig made a rumbling sound in his throat which might have signified discontent, or perhaps heartburn.

"I planned to go down to the station today," he said, as rain began to fall against the windshield. Lightly at first, then in great, fat drops that fell like pebbles against the glass. "Niall said, if I was to think of anything else, I should mention it."

Gregory turned to him, all business now.

"What have you remembered, Padraig?"

"Probably not important," the other man said. "But I was varnishing one of the dinghies the morning Claire Kelly died. It's an outdoor job—smelly one, too. Anyway, I was down at the shoreline, by the boathouse, and I saw that feller from the school."

"Tom Reilly?" Gregory asked, with a frown.

"Aye, the headmaster. He was out for a jog. I could see him, up on the lough trail. Always wears those tight shorts and headphones that look like bloody earmuffs. Remember thinkin' he belongs in Dublin, decked out like that. Anyway, I told Niall that nobody could give me an alibi for that morning—but I thought it might be worth asking Reilly whether he remembers seeing me, varnishing the boat, like."

"Thanks for telling me."

"As I said, probably not important now they've got Connor in their sights. You think I should still mention it to that new superintendent?"

Gregory nodded.

"They need every detail, no matter how small."

As they continued on to the hotel, he was left with the overpowering impression that he'd just been gifted an important piece of the jigsaw puzzle, if only he could figure out where it went.

It was just before six when Alex returned to his room in the hotel and ate a solitary, room-service dinner. The wind continued to pick up, howling through the chimney piece and rattling the old windows as the storm finally took hold of Ballyfinny. When he looked outside, he saw the skies had changed from the watercolour pinks and mauves of earlier, and were now a deepening grey-blue, as night fell behind the clouds.

Unable to settle, he picked up the case file which still sat on his desk. He'd remember to take it back to the Garda the following day but, until then, it couldn't do any harm to thumb through the old paperwork, one more time.

When he looked again at the crime scene photographs of Claire Kelly, he found himself thinking of the precise location of the Kelly house. He recalled seeing the entrance to one of the woodland pathways that ran down to a jetty by the lough, and realised that the lough trail which ran all the way around the water must also pass by the bottom of the dead woman's house.

It was the same route taken by Tom Reilly to get to the shoreline where he'd been seen by Padraig—and the same route he could have taken back into town, passing close to Connor's hut. It must have taken at least an hour to jog the full circuit; more, depending on his level of fitness.

He sat perfectly still for all of five minutes, and then made a grab for the phone.

But the number he dialled was busy, as was the next.

He tried the Garda Station in Ballyfinny, but there was no answer. It was after six, and their out-of-town officers had been told to go home early, in light of the yellow weather warning. They'd taken the time to leave an answer machine message, which told him cheerfully to 'leave a message after the beep'. He tried all the numbers again and, when there was still no reply, decided there was no time to lose and slammed the phone back into its cradle.

He made for the door at a run.

CHAPTER 37

When Gregory stepped outside the hotel, the wind hit him like a slap in the face.

He ran full pelt across the lawn towards the trees on the far side, feeling the air sting his skin, so cold it burned. Fear was a living, breathing thing inside him, and he battled to keep it at bay as he dived into the trees and made for the pathway that would take him past the tennis courts and towards the town centre. Pine cones scattered as he half-walked, half-ran through the forest, keeping to the worn pathway. The trees rose up all around him, like silent sentinels that seemed to contract and move.

It's only your mind, playing tricks again.

There, beneath the forest canopy, he could have been anywhere in the world. With only Nature as his companion, it might have been ten, twenty or even a hundred years ago, and the landscape would have looked much the same as it did then. It was as though Alex had stepped into a kind of ether; a halfway place, or No-Man's Land, with only himself and his demons as a guide.

They're only projections, he told himself. *Not real anymore.*

He heard his breathing quicken and saw it cloud on the air before disappearing again, swallowed up by the surrounding darkness.

Suddenly, there came a flash of lightning piercing the sky, followed immediately by a deafening rumble that seemed to shake the very foundations of the trees.

The storm had come.

Thoughts of the red-headed woman were all consuming, now.

For a long time, it had been possible to think of other things; to imagine other women.

Other mothers.

But that time had passed, and it was impossible to imagine anyone else. Nobody else would do.

Closing their eyes, they could picture her in the house by the water, reading by the fire. She liked to do that, more often than television these days, and chose a book for herself from the pitiful selection at Ballyfinny Library most Saturdays. They were always the same, too; thin, romance volumes with pictures of men and women on the front, lost in the heat of passion.

Lies, lies, lies.

She enjoyed living the lie. She liked to pretend, just as much as they did.

Maggie had never felt so tired.

It ran all the way through to her bones, as she moved slowly around the cottage, without energy or purpose. When she'd lost Aiden all those years ago, and cried until there were no more tears left, she'd kept going because there had been Niall and then Connor to think of. She'd carried on taking air into her lungs, breathing in and out, putting one leg in front of the other all the hours of the day until night came around again, and the empty space beside her on the bed beckoned her to a restless, lonely sleep. Each day passed the same way, until they rolled into weeks and then months, and her children grew so tall and strong, they no longer needed her to hold their hands or fight their battles. She'd woken up to find herself a woman of sixty, with lines on her face and hair that was no longer auburn but steel grey.

She hardly recognised herself, this pale imitation of a woman she'd once known.

That had been three years ago. Since then, she'd vowed to make every year count, and had thrown herself into civic duty and caring for her grandchild with the kind of gusto that would have made Aiden's head spin.

"*Go easy, girl,*" he used to say. "*We've all the time in the world.*"

But, in the end, there had been no more time for him; just as there was no more time for Claire Kelly, nor Aideen and Colm McArdle.

Perhaps, soon, there would be no more time for her.

———

Gregory was shivering badly. The weatherproof jacket he wore was not thick enough to shelter him from his own nightmares, which rose to the surface of his mind to taunt him as he hurried onward through the trees.

Where are you going, Alex?

"To help," he muttered.

You can't help them all, the voice whispered. *You couldn't help me.*

"I'm trying," he said. "I'm trying to help you."

He thought he caught a glimpse of a woman walking up ahead, just the flash of a face, and he began to run—harder, faster, until his muscles ached, and the wind screamed in his ears.

You're too late again.

He heard the voice and wanted to stop, but he didn't. He couldn't stop now.

He knew who was going to be next.

———

The red-headed woman would still be reading, at this hour.

She'd be sitting in her chair by the fire or getting into the fancy little roll-top bath she liked so much. They'd seen her, getting undressed and looking at herself in the mirror, prodding her hips and patting the loose skin of her belly, where a child had once been.

She'd climb into the bath and pick up her book again, escaping into a world of make-believe where she could pretend to be the heroine, the saviour, the lover.

But never the mother.

Never that.

———

When Alex reached the edge of the forest, he sucked great, gulping breaths of air into his lungs. The rain beat more heavily against his brow without the trees to shelter him, but he welcomed the deluge and held his face up to the eye of the storm, letting it cleanse his skin and his mind before hurrying onward.

Not far now.

Thunder rocked the small town as he ran through its empty streets and, when he reached the hilly incline leading up to Maggie's cottage, he raced upwards, never stopping until he reached her door.

CHAPTER 38

The loud banging at her front door made Maggie jump, spilling hot tea over the back of her hand.

"Bugger and blast," she muttered, and rinsed it beneath the cold tap as the banging grew even more insistent. "I'll be there in a minute!"

Emma was at home with Declan, and Niall had stayed on at Castlebar while Connor was held for further questioning. Seamus was unlikely to leave the hotel, nor Padraig in the bad weather. That only left—

"I might have known it'd be you," she said, when she opened the door to find Alex standing there. His clothes were soaked through and he had a wild, urgent look about him.

He didn't wait to be asked, but barged straight in, where he began to roam through the downstairs rooms.

"What the—hey! Hold up a minute, there, lad. Niall isn't here, if you're looking for him. He's on his way back from Castlebar. He's taken the longer road, most likely, with the weather being as it is. I can make you a cup of tea, if you want to wait."

Alex was troubled.

"It isn't him I'm looking for," he muttered. "Where's Emma?"

"She's at home, looking after Declan," Maggie said, in confusion. "What can you want with her?"

"Is she on her own?" he asked, ignoring the question.

Maggie nodded.

"As far as I know," she said. "Why?"

Gregory ran a hand over his face and came to a quick decision.

"I need the truth from you, Maggie. I already know that, on Friday nights, you look after Declan. You usually have him on Saturday mornings, too. But I need you to tell me where Niall goes."

"I don't—" she began.

"It's important."

Something in his eyes must have convinced her.

"He goes to Alcoholics Anonymous," she said, and was glad to get it off her chest. "He didn't want anyone in Ballyfinny or Castlebar to know, so he goes across to Galway instead. Sometimes, Connor drives him down. Niall only told me last night. There'll be no more wine at my dinner table from now on, I can tell you that."

Gregory closed his eyes, as the final piece slotted neatly into place.

"Call him now, Maggie. Tell him he needs to go straight home."

"He's already on the road," she said. "That's where he'll be heading, anyhow."

"Where do Emma and Niall live?"

She gave the address to him and, seconds later, he was heading for the door.

"Wait! Where are you going? What's all this about?" she demanded.

"We need to get to Emma and Declan, as quickly as we can."

Maggie didn't need to be told twice. She shoved her feet into a pair of old slippers and grabbed her coat from the peg.

"I'll drive," she said, and they hurried back out into the rain.

Niall and Emma Byrne lived in a converted barn, only a couple of streets away from the McArdle house. When Maggie's car pulled up outside, they found the curtains drawn at each of the windows.

"Do you have a key?" Gregory asked, and was already out of the car before she'd pulled the hand brake.

"Yes, I've got one, here," she said, hurrying around the other side of the car. "Try ringing the bell, first."

He rang the bell and, when there was no answer, hammered the painted wood with his fist.

"Dear God, you don't think—"

Gregory hammered again, harder this time.

When there was still no answer, he peered through the letterbox to the dim hallway beyond, then stood back to allow Maggie to open the door.

Once they were inside, Alex held up a protective hand to indicate she should stay well back. He cursed himself for not thinking to bring anything he could use as a weapon, before remembering that his words were his greatest weapon of all.

"Be careful," he told her, and took his first step into the unknown.

Around now, she'd be sitting on the sofa, smiling at something she'd read in her book, while the light from the fire picked up the copper tone of her hair. It wasn't natural, of course; not any more. But, once, it had been.

Once.

That was a funny word; something had happened *once*, and they remembered being told never to repeat it to another living soul.

But it was never just the '*once*'.

It had been every week, then every other night.

And it was always while the woman with the red hair read her romance stories on the sofa by the fire.

Alex and Maggie made a full search of the downstairs, but found nothing.

The lights were on, but nobody seemed to be home.

"She might have popped out somewhere, with Declan," Maggie offered, but the sense of panic was rising sharply in her chest.

It was not like Emma to take Declan anywhere so late.

"I'll check upstairs," Gregory said.

Maggie followed behind him and they mounted the creaking staircase with its gallery wall of family photographs, all carefully arranged in different sizes.

We're a happy family! it screamed.

At the top of the stairs, Alex checked every room, until he came to the one at the end of the corridor. It was painted white, as they all were, and had a small hanging sign that said 'DECLAN' in the shape of a dinosaur. It stood ajar, and they could see the swirling colours of the little boy's night light projected against the ceiling, as it played a soft lullaby.

Gregory's stomach trembled as he approached the doorway, never more afraid than he was then. Maggie's breath was coming in short pants as she fought to stay calm, and he deliberately angled his body so he would be the first to see whatever lay waiting for them.

He pushed open the door.

Declan lay sprawled on his bed, one arm hanging off the edge, his face turned into the pillow.

"Oh, sweet Jesus!" Maggie cried out, and Alex ran inside to check for a pulse. "Is he dead? Oh, God, please, no—"

He found a pulse, but it was thin.

"He's alive."

Maggie sank to her knees and laid a shaking hand on her grandson's hair, murmuring a prayer of thanks.

"Why—why isn't he waking up?" she asked, and wiped the tears from her eyes with the back of her sleeve.

"I don't know," Gregory said honestly, still checking the boy's pulse against the watch on his wrist. "He's breathing, but seems to be comatose. He may just be in a deep sleep. Is it hard to wake him, usually?"

"No, never," Maggie replied. "He's a light sleeper, as a rule."

"It may be drug-induced," Gregory said. "Sleeping pills, cough medicine, or something of that sort."

That had been Cathy Jones' favourite medley, he recalled. The toxicology report following the death of her baby girl had eventually thrown up a cocktail of ingredients to make her permanently drowsy, usually found in high street cough medicine. Mix it with a soupçon of table salt, and you had quite a recipe for disaster.

He looked down at the boy's sleeping body and felt something lift inside his heart.

You could save some of them, after all.

"I'll call an ambulance," he said. "You stay with him, and—"

He fell silent as he heard the sound of a key turning in the lock downstairs. He exchanged a glance with Maggie, who lifted her grandson in gentle arms and held him against her chest.

If anyone had come to hurt him, they would need to get past her, first.

CHAPTER 39

Inspector Niall Byrne let himself into the house, but didn't bother to announce it. There had been a time, years ago, when he'd have called out to Emma and Declan, and she'd have called out a cheerful 'hello' and come to the door to greet him—but not now. Things were different, and it was hard, so hard, not to remember how things used to be.

Being married to a police detective was no walk in the park. There were long hours and late nights to contend with, and, even when he was at home, it was hard not to bring some of the job home with him. How could he make light and chat about everyday nonsense, when he was faced with the very worst of society each day? Until recently, the people of Ballyfinny had been unaccustomed to violent crime, and the worst they ever needed to contend with was the occasional bit of petty theft, or light assault between a couple of old duffers down at O'Feeney's on a Friday night. Connor managed the town well, and he respected his brother for the efforts he made to use the law proportionately. A young person might wind up in jail, otherwise, and then all hope would be lost. But, at divisional level, he was faced with more serious crime—more drugs-related theft and violence, more prostitution, rapes and murders.

And then, he came home to Ballyfinny and was expected to talk about parking misdemeanours.

In Dublin, Emma had understood. She had her own circle of teacher friends, and her own life, so he never had to hide the darkness he sometimes saw in his. They had been evenly matched. He couldn't tell precisely when things had begun to go wrong, but perhaps it had been the move home to Ballyfinny. Rural life was not for everyone, and some preferred the bright lights of the city. She was still grieving the death of her father, as well as being on hand to help her mother to come to terms with the loss, which took its toll.

There was no intimacy any more.

At first, he'd believed the excuses about her being tired, or having headaches, and because he loved her, it would never occur to him to push or pressure her. He'd tried to help her through the grieving process, to offer his shoulder if she needed it, but Emma preferred not to talk about it.

It was as though she had completely closed in on herself.

The only time he saw a spark of the woman he'd married was when she was with Declan. There was never a gentler, kinder woman than Emma, when it came to their son. It gave him some comfort to know that, but he couldn't help the small darts of jealousy he felt, watching them together. It made him ashamed to admit that, even to himself.

And then there was his drinking.

At least that was something he was trying to change. Maybe, then, Emma might look at him the way she used to.

Even the thought of alcohol made his throat dry, so he busied himself taking off his jacket and tie, and was about to go off in search of his wife when he heard a creak on the stairs. However, when he looked up, it was not Emma who joined him in the hallway, but Doctor Gregory.

"What the hell are you doing here?"

Alex held his hands up, and answered quickly.

"Your mother's upstairs, with Declan," he said. "Niall, I need you to stay calm. Declan is unwell, and we've called an ambulance. Emma isn't here."

The inspector turned pale, and looked over Gregory's shoulder, towards the stairs.

"God, no—don't tell me?"

Niall pushed past Alex and took the stairs two at a time, calling for his wife and child. Gregory left the front door ajar for the paramedics and then ran after him, to find Niall crouched beside his son's bed. Maggie still lay with Declan in her arms, stroking his sleeping head with a gentle hand, and Gregory held back while the man leant across to kiss his son's cheek. Niall swiped a shirtsleeve over his eyes and pressed his face to his mother's shoulder, who rocked them both and sang an Irish love song beneath her breath.

Gregory felt his stomach twist and he turned away, leaning his head back against the wall to stare at the ceiling until the feeling passed.

Niall left Declan to his mother's safekeeping, and found Gregory waiting for him in the hallway.

"The paramedics will be here as soon as they can," Alex said, to give the man some comfort. "He's in good hands until then."

"Where's Emma?"

"She's with her mother," Gregory said softly. "We need to find her, as soon as possible. It can't wait."

Niall fought a battle between comprehension and confusion.

"I don't understand," he said. "Why would she leave Declan alone?"

Gregory put a hand on the man's arm.

"Emma lied to me—she told me she'd been having an affair with Tom Reilly and was with him the morning Claire Kelly died. I thought she was giving him an alibi, but she was really trying to set one up for herself. We need to get to her mother's house, right away. There's no time, Niall. It may already be too late."

The other man's eyes were dark with misery, and then horror, as broken images from the crime scenes began to run through his mind, like an old-fashioned show reel.

Not Emma.

It can't be…

"Mary lives on the other side of the lough," he said, speaking robotically. "In one of the villages."

"I'll drive," Gregory offered, and started to leave, but Niall stopped him.

"Wait—you can't. The lough road's been closed after a flood, and it's the quickest route."

"What's the alternative?"

Niall speared both hands through his hair while he tried to think, to get past the waves of shock that rocked his system.

"Ah, there's a longer route via the main roads," he said. "Takes twice the time, but it'd be the only other option by car."

He swung around to look for Emma's keys, and found them gone.

"I probably passed her, on the road coming home," he said, in a monotone.

Gregory put a hand on his arm, to bring his attention back.

"Is there any other way?"

Niall shook his head.

"There's no other way on the roads. She's already got a head start on us; if we leave now, we'd be too late."

Alex swore softly.

"Unless—we could take a boat…" Niall said.

The two men looked at each other, then at the raging storm outside, howling against the windowpanes.

"At least it's not an aeroplane," Gregory muttered. "Where do we find one?"

Niall's face was set into determined lines.

"Connor's hut."

CHAPTER 40

The two men left at a run, and didn't stop until they reached Connor's hut.

The rain was coming down in sheets, saturating their clothes and shoes, but they neither noticed nor cared. The water level was high on the lough, and Connor's boat bobbed precariously on the choppy waves, its rudder tapping against the wooden jetty.

"We need a key!" Niall shouted, his voice carrying on the wind.

Gregory didn't hesitate but tore through the plastic Garda line barring the entrance to the fishing hut and, when the door wouldn't give, planted his boot and give it a couple of hard kicks. If Niall was surprised, he said nothing, and while Alex began searching the disordered space for boat keys, he put a call through to Superintendent Donoghue.

The phone answered after several attempts.

"Donoghue?"

"This better be good," she told him. "I'm at home with my family, Niall. I've told you, we'll consider a petition for Connor's bail in the morning—"

"We know who it is," Niall said, but couldn't bring himself to say her name.

"What?"

Niall brought her up to speed, and Donoghue agreed to send an army of squad cars to the address.

"No helicopter will go out in this weather," she said, "and the lough road's impassable. The earliest they'll be able to get there is forty-five minutes, and that's thinking optimistically. Niall, I'm ordering you to stand down."

Inspector Byrne thought of the woman on the other side of the lough, who was the mother of his child. He thought of the other women she had killed, and would kill again, if he did nothing. He looked down at the smartphone in his hand and, very carefully, ended the call.

Gregory jiggled some keys.

"Only ones I could find," he said. "Did you get through to Donoghue?"

"She's sending reinforcements, but they won't be able to get there for a while."

He looked out across the lough, whose waters crashed against the shore, and then back at Gregory.

"We're on our own."

Gregory had sailed plenty of times before. That is, if you counted taking a pedalo around the headland of a Greek island in the height of summer, or rowing a pretty girl across the Serpentine in Hyde Park at springtime. The reality of his present situation was a world away from those pleasant memories, and he gripped the edges of the tiny fishing boat with white knuckles.

There had been times in his life when he'd been afraid, but now he knew real *fear*. The kind that came only from staring death in the eye and entertaining the possibility it could claim you, with one wrong move.

Niall gunned the boat's engine, but it struggled against the force of the waves, its propeller growling and spluttering as it chugged slowly across the rolling waters. He felt his stomach heave as the bow of the boat reared up, where it was suspended for an endless moment, before crashing down again.

Alex manned a lever at the bow, the muscles in his arm burning as he worked to pump water from the bottom of the boat and back into the lough. It was a losing battle against the force of the storm, but he continued to fight it while the spray blinded him, and the waves tossed the little wooden boat from side to side.

Teeth gritted, bodily exhausted, they skirted around the headland, pushing the boat onwards through dark waters where jagged rocks lay hidden, until a small cluster of lights appeared up ahead.

"There!" Niall shouted, and fought the power of the waves to bring the boat around.

The boat overturned as they were coming into a small inlet nearest to the village of Innishmore, where Emma's mother lived. The first shock of the water stole the breath from their bodies, while the current dragged them under and spun them around, so they were no longer sure which way was up. There was no daylight to guide them, and they took in mouthfuls of water as they struggled to find the surface.

When he did, Gregory opened his mouth to take in air, but was immediately bombarded by another rolling wave which battered his body and sent him crashing against the side of the upturned boat. He made a weak grab for the side and held on with all his strength, heaving water from his lungs while his legs worked to keep him upright.

When he was able, he tried to call out to Niall, but heard nothing over the sound of the water.

But, in the reflected light of the village, he thought he saw an arm rising up to the surface, flailing around before falling under again.

He pushed away from the boat and struck off in that direction, arms and legs screaming, until he spotted Niall. With one last push, he made a grab for the other man and held on for grim life.

They were shaking and shivering when they washed up on the small shingle beach at Innishmore. Alex rose up on all fours and vomited water before collapsing back against the pebbles, while Niall dragged himself across and took a fistful of his shirt.

"Thank you," he said, hoarsely.

"Don't mention it," Gregory wheezed, and then ordered his body to move.

Move!

The water was freezing, and so were they.

"C'mon," he said, dragging himself up again. "We need to keep moving."

By the time they stumbled off the beach, they were both shaking badly.

"Which way?" Gregory demanded, rubbing furiously at his arms to warm them. "We need to find some dry clothes."

"Mary will have some at the house," Niall said. "It isn't far."

It took less than two minutes to reach the cottage where Emma grew up. Like many in the area, it was small and boxy in construction, white-washed with a traditional thatched roof. From the outside, there was nothing to cause them any alarm, and Emma's car was nowhere to be seen.

"Maybe we beat her to it," Niall said, and might have cried.

She was already the enemy.

"Or, she could have parked elsewhere. She was planning to go out and be back before you got home, leaving Declan to sleep. She wouldn't want to park her car here for someone to witness."

As they approached, Niall paused.

"You take the back, I'll take the front. It'll cut off her escape route."

"Niall? When you speak to her, tell her that you understand."

"I don't," he said. "I *can't*. She's murdered two people—"

"Don't think of her as the Emma you want her to be, think of her as a woman whose mind is broken. That might help, when the time comes."

The other man nodded.

"She'll feel threatened, Niall. I don't think she'll attack, but when she sees you, she'll know it's all over and there's nothing to lose. That changes the perspective. She might harm herself, or you; maybe both. Be careful."

"And you, Doc."

CHAPTER 41

It might have been September everywhere else in the world, but it was Christmastime inside Mary Callaghan's cottage. The large, artificial tree she usually kept in the attic until the first of December had been set up in its usual spot by the bay window, decked with baubles and tinsel. Beneath the tree, there was a nativity scene and little presents, carefully wrapped. Bing Crosby sang from an old CD player, and *Home Alone* played silently on the television next to a large wicker basket embroidered with a teddy bear.

Mary was lying on the sofa, rendered unconscious by a single blow to the head.

Beside her, a smart red dress had been laid out in readiness; the one she always wore during the festive season because it had been her husband's favourite.

While she slept, her daughter baked in the kitchen.

Emma hadn't bothered to wear the coveralls she'd taken from the boot of Connor's car. She was protected here, where the Garda would expect to find her prints and DNA, but she would take extra precautions once Ma got changed for dinner.

Ladies always changed for dinner. That's what her mother used to tell her.

She looked over at the dining table, which had been laid for two using the china her mother usually reserved 'for best'. There were crackers and Christmas napkins, and candles all around. A golden turkey sat in the centre, still hot from the oven, and the vegetables were almost done.

"Nearly ready, Ma!" she called out, and reached across for the heavy, five-inch carving knife in her mother's block. "I hope you're hungry."

She turned off the cooker and hob, checked everything was in place, and then washed her hands.

Cleanliness was next to Godliness.

That's what her father used to say.

Niall let himself into the cottage very slowly, preparing himself for an attack at any moment. If he allowed himself to think about it, about Emma and what she had done, he would fold.

He had sworn to protect.

He had vowed to love her in sickness, and in health.

When he slipped into the living room and saw the decorations, his first reaction was to wonder how long she had left their young son drugged and alone in order to set up her bastardised celebration.

Anger was raw, and visceral, but he told himself to remain calm.

Secure the scene.

He spotted his mother-in-law on the sofa, and hurried across the room to check she was breathing. A deep gash to the side of her temple was weeping onto the cushion beside her, but she was still alive.

There was no time to take cover before Emma walked back into the room. She wore a Christmas jumper he'd given her a few years ago, and carried a large carving knife by her side. She stopped dead when she saw him standing there, cold and shivering.

Time seemed to stand still while husband and wife regarded each other.

"You weren't invited," she said, in a funny, high-pitched voice.

He searched her face for any sign of the woman he loved, but saw only an impostor.

"It's time to go back, Emma," he said. "You need to come with me, now."

"Not until we've eaten Christmas lunch," she said, stubbornly. "Mammy says we can open our presents after lunch."

Niall was out of his depth, floundering deep in something he didn't understand, when he spotted Gregory slipping through the back door and into the dining room, behind where Emma stood.

"What did you put on your Christmas list?" he asked, and she spun around, raising the knife as if to attack.

"You're not going to hurt anybody with that, Emma."

He held eye contact, and spoke slowly and clearly.

"I understand that you don't want to hurt me, Emma—or Niall, or yourself."

She sobbed, and shook her head.

"I understand you don't really want to hurt your mother either," he said, and she swayed on the spot, looking down at the knife in her hand and then over her shoulder to where Mary was lying on the sofa.

"What happened, Emma? Will you tell me?"

She sobbed again, and the knife lowered a fraction. Behind her, Niall took a careful step closer.

"I can't," she whispered.

A promise is a promise, her father used to say.

"Did somebody hurt you, Emma?"

The woman seemed to have abandoned her body, leaving only a child behind. Gregory spoke to the child, now, and not the woman who had murdered three people—and attempted a fourth.

"Daddy said not to tell."

Niall let out a small sound of shock and sadness, and she turned on him, raising the knife once again.

"Stay back!" she screamed. "Don't you come near me!"

Gregory wondered whether she saw Niall, or the father who had died.

"He's gone, Emma," he said. "He won't hurt you anymore."

But she was shaking her head, and gripping the knife tightly.

"It was Christmas," she whispered, looking across to where her mother had begun to stir. "She *knew,* and she did nothing. She did nothing at all."

"I understand, Emma," Niall said, remembering Gregory's advice.

She turned to him and smiled, her face softening back into the woman he'd loved; whose hand he'd held at the altar, and on the delivery table.

"Thank you," she whispered.

Gregory saw the flash of movement, and lunged forward as the blade swept up to her throat.

CHAPTER 42

Not long after, Gregory stood outside Mary Callaghan's cottage in Innishmore, watching while her daughter was transferred into a waiting ambulance, under Garda supervision. His interception had been timely, and the knife had only caught the surface of her neck, leaving an angry red line rather than severing the arteries beneath. He knew there would be some who might say that death would have been the better option; the same people who believed in taking an eye for an eye. But, as somebody had once said, if everybody took that attitude, the whole world would end up blind. Somewhere inside the shell of Emma Byrne, there had been a loving mother and wife, a good friend and a productive member of society. Unfortunately, a small, crucial part of her had been broken, and the wound had never healed. It had festered instead, and the gangrene left to spread until it obliterated the woman she might once have been.

He looked over to where Niall was giving his statement to Superintendent Donoghue and couldn't help but admire the man's fortitude. There would be months and years of trauma to deal with; denials, tears and, finally, acceptance that he was not to blame for his wife's actions. When she went through the court process, others would decide whether she was of sound mind but, whether she lived out her days in a prison or in a secure hospital, she must live with the consequences of taking a life.

A few minutes later, Niall walked over to join him.

"How're you holding up?" Gregory asked.

"It seems unreal," he replied. "Yesterday, she was Emma. My wife. Now—"

He fell silent, and they watched the ambulance doors close.

"She wanted me to go with her to the hospital," he said. "And a part of me wanted to go, but I just can't. I can hardly look at her."

Horror, betrayal, pity...it was all there, Gregory thought.

"Nobody expects it of you," he murmured. "There's no 'right' or 'wrong' answer."

Niall nodded.

"The signs were there," he muttered. "All the things you said in your profile—right there in front of me, and I never even thought of her."

"Why would you?" Gregory countered. "She's your wife."

"All the same, there were signs," he said. "She couldn't stand to be touched. Started having nightmares, violent terrors, and lashing out if I tried to help. Looking back, it all began after her father died. You said there'd be a trigger."

Alex nodded.

"She wished her mother could have been more like Claire, or Aideen. She wanted a chance to relive her childhood as she wanted it to be, not how it really was. The true source of her anger had already died without any resolution, so her mother became the main focus. It takes courage to act on the darkest of fantasies, and she built it up by killing the others first."

"I don't know how I'll ever face their families," he said, and dropped his head into his hands. "Liam, Emily…they were our friends—"

"You're a victim and a survivor, too," Gregory said. "Don't forget that. You weren't the perpetrator, Niall. You were the one to bring an end to this."

The other man looked up at the sky, which was dark and forbidding as the storm raged on.

"We're in for more rain," he said.

"Doesn't seem so bad, when you've swallowed half a gallon of lough water," Gregory replied, and brought a reluctant smile to the inspector's face.

He had one more thing he needed to say, before he went home to his son.

"Thank you for stopping her," he said. "I was out of reach, but you could have held back, or not bothered at all. But, even after everything she's done, I wouldn't wish it."

Gregory thought again of the many different kinds of people in the world, and then turned to shake the man's hand.

"You've got my number, Niall. If you ever need to talk, about anything at all, you know where I am."

For once, there were no jokes about head-doctors or mind-readers.

"Thanks, Doc."

CHAPTER 43

Monday

The storm had broken in the early hours of the morning, heralding the dawn of a bright new day. In keeping with the best traditions of Irish hospitality, a small crowd had gathered in the bar at the Ballyfinny Castle Hotel to bid Alex farewell, before he braved the flight from Knock Airport to London for a final time.

"*Sláinte is táinte,*" Connor said, and raised his glass. "To your health and wealth, Doc."

"Cheers," Gregory said, and knocked back the last of his drink. "I guess it'll be back to bar brawls and meetings with the Neighbourhood Watch, for you?"

Connor grinned.

"That's a full-time occupation, around these parts."

Alex returned his grin.

"I hope you weren't planning to sneak off without a proper 'goodbye'?"

He turned at the sound of Maggie's voice. The Mayor of Ballyfinny looked exhausted, and her eyes were dimmed by sadness, but it hadn't prevented her from making a public address that morning, nor from coming to see him off.

He thought, not for the first time, that she was quite a lady.

"It's been no bed of roses, but I'm glad to have met you, Alex," she said, casting a maternal eye over the shadows beneath his eyes. There was something else, she thought. Some indefinable quality that set him apart from the rest of the world. "Thanks for everything."

"I meant what I said, yesterday. Your family are lucky to have you."

Caught off-guard, she blinked furiously.

"There, now. You're a good lad. Your Ma must be proud."

Gregory said nothing, but smiled and reached down to brush his lips against her cheek.

"Take care of yourself, Lady Mayor."

Gregory settled himself into the passenger seat of Padraig's newly-refurbished Land Rover and looked across at his designated driver for the trip; a man who had clearly never kissed the Blarney Stone in all his life.

"Ready?" he asked.

"As I'll ever be," Gregory replied.

The car took off with a roar, leading him to wonder whether Padraig had added a little extra spice to the engine, when he'd rebuilt it.

"Weather's turned," Alex said, to get the ball rolling.

"Aye."

"I wonder if Ireland will win, at the rugby."

Padraig grunted.

"You know, I'm going to miss these little chats of ours," Gregory said.

"I've heard it said that silence is golden," Padraig replied.

"In that case, you must shit solid gold nuggets," Gregory threw back.

They exchanged an appreciative smile, and passed the rest of the journey in a companionable silence.

EPILOGUE

Thursday
Southmoor Hospital, London

Alex used the remainder of his leave to visit Bill Douglas in Cambridge, where he found himself agreeing to accompany his friend to a conference on 'Criminal Profiling and the Police', to be held in Paris. It was no hardship to visit that beautiful city, but Alex was never more aware that with every acceptance, he fell further down the rabbit hole and back into the seductive realms of investigative profiling. To counteract the feeling, he was glad to return to his desk at Southmoor Hospital, and to fall back into a regular routine of patients and clinical care meetings, which included his regular Thursday afternoon session with Cathy Jones.

However, when the allotted time came and went without any sign of her, Gregory set aside his notepad and went off in search of answers.

His footsteps tapped a staccato rhythm against the floor as he made his way through a series of air-locked security doors separating his office and the residential ward where Cathy Jones lived.

But, when he looked through the Perspex window, he found her room stripped bare.

He unlocked the door and stepped inside, searching the space for any sign that she had once been there. Aside from the faintest scent of floral perfume still hanging on the air, there was nothing.

Gregory walked swiftly towards the Clinical Director's office, almost giving in to the temptation to run, but mindful of the rules they lived by in that secure environment.

When he reached a door bearing a small brass plaque engraved, 'DR PARMINDER AGGARWAL', he knocked briskly.

"Come in!"

The Clinical Director was a thin woman with a big smile, who managed to project an air of boundless energy and enthusiasm; a characteristic that was highly desirable in a place like Southmoor, where the spectre of anti-psychotic medications and violent patients could take the shine off anybody's day, and where cheerfulness was often in short supply.

"Hi, Alex," she said, smiling broadly. "Good to see you back from your travels. How was Ireland?"

But he was in no mood for small talk.

"Thanks, it's good to be back. Actually, I wanted to ask you about a patient of mine, who I was expecting to see for a session this afternoon—Cathy Jones? She didn't turn up, and

I've just been along to check her room and found it empty. Has she been transferred to another facility?"

Aggarwal removed the preposterously large glasses she wore, and rubbed the bridge of her nose.

"Ah, yes. I'm sorry, you wouldn't have heard, since you were away. I'm afraid we lost Cathy, in the early hours of Monday morning."

In the ensuing silence, Gregory realised she was expecting a response from him.

"I'm sorry to hear that. Do you mind if I read the Incident Report?" he asked, and then cleared his throat. "How—ah, how did it happen?"

"It seems she managed to get hold of some rosary beads, which she used to hang herself," Aggarwal explained. "We're still trying to find out how she came by them. I'll be interviewing the rest of the care staff today and tomorrow."

Gregory nodded in the right places, and made all the right noises. Then, when an acceptable amount of time had passed, he excused himself.

"I haven't been able to find a next of kin," Aggarwal said, before he reached the door. "In her case, there was a husband and three children, wasn't there?"

"Divorced," Gregory supplied. "The husband re-married, twice. She had three children, but two died by her hand."

"And the third?"

"Leave it to me," he said.

Alex didn't think of it again until he had returned to the privacy of his own home, on the banks of the Thames. With slow and precise movements, he turned and locked his front door, then drew up the chair he kept beside it and tucked it beneath the handle, to be doubly sure.

He stood in the middle of the living room and closed his eyes, drowning out the sounds of the city that were normally so comforting.

But not today.

He moved to the spare room he used as an office, and pulled a key from a small locked box he kept in one of the filing cabinets, before retrieving a larger locked box he kept on the bottom shelf of his wardrobe.

The box gave nothing away about the enormity of its contents, being a plain, black metal affair with a silver lock. He sank down onto the edge of his bed and set it on his lap, giving himself a moment to prepare before unlocking it.

Inside, there was a stack of papers, photographs and small trinkets salvaged from his early years. His fingers hovered above it, wary even to touch the physical evidence of who he had once been. Eventually, he sifted through the papers until he found a birth certificate, yellowed with age, belonging to the boy who had been Michael Alexander Jones, eldest son of Cathy.

He passed over Change of Name documents and court papers, until he came to the only photograph he'd chosen to keep of them all together. It had been taken sometime in the weeks after his sister Emily was born, and showed a mother, a father and three smiling children sitting on the lawn of a large country house near Richmond, in one of London's most affluent suburbs.

It was, perhaps, the last happy memory he had of his mother.

Alex shoved the papers onto the bed and stood up again, moving directly to the window overlooking the river. He opened it and stood there for a long time, watching the people passing by, listening to the sound of the city where he'd been born.

He thought back to the day his mother's name had appeared on the list of new patients at Southmoor Hospital, and of the choice he'd made. All his life, he had wondered *why*. He'd followed a career in psychology to try to understand the workings of the human mind, all the while hoping it might bring him closer to understanding the woman who'd given him life.

Then, one day, she was presented to him as a patient.

It seemed like a gift; a perfect opportunity to understand his mother's motivations, directly from the source. He could ask her all the questions he'd longed to ask, and be given all the answers that would help him to forgive her.

She'd never given him any answers, but he'd held onto the hope that, one day, she would improve. Just enough to show even one moment of remorse.

Now, she never would.

Alex Gregory will return in—

HYSTERIA

In a beautiful world, murder is always ugly…

Recently returned from his last case in Ireland, elite forensic psychologist and criminal profiler Dr Alexander Gregory receives a call from the French police that he can't ignore. It's Paris fashion week and some of the world's most beautiful women are turning up dead, their faces slashed in a series of frenzied attacks while the world's press looks on.

Amidst the carnage, one victim has survived but she's too traumatised to talk. Without her help, the police are powerless to stop the killer before he strikes again—can Gregory unlock the secrets of her mind, before it's too late?

Murder and mystery are peppered with dark humour in this fast-paced thriller set amidst the spectacular Parisian landscape.

Don't miss book #2 of the Alexander Gregory Thrillers— available in all good bookshops from December 2019!

ABOUT THE AUTHOR

LJ Ross is an international bestselling author, best known for creating atmospheric mystery and thriller novels, including the DCI Ryan series of Northumbrian murder mysteries which have sold over seven million copies worldwide.

Her debut, *Holy Island,* was released in January 2015 and reached number one in the UK and Australian charts. Since then, she has released more than twenty further novels, all of which have been top three global bestsellers and almost all of which have been UK #1 bestsellers. Louise has garnered an army of loyal readers through her storytelling and, thanks to them, many of her books reached the coveted #1 spot whilst only available to pre-order ahead of release.

Louise was born in Northumberland, England. She studied undergraduate and postgraduate Law at King's College, University of London and then abroad in

Paris and Florence. She spent much of her working life in London, where she was a lawyer for a number of years until taking the decision to change career and pursue her dream to write. Now, she writes full time and lives with her family in Northumberland. She enjoys reading all manner of books, travelling and spending time with family and friends.

If you enjoyed this book, please consider leaving a review online.

If you would like to be kept up to date with new releases from LJ Ross, please complete an e-mail contact form on her Facebook page or website, www.ljrossauthor.com

Scan the QR code below to find out more
about LJ Ross and her books

ACKNOWLEDGMENTS

My interest in psychology was first sparked by my lovely mum, Susan, who was (and is still) a psychologist herself. I remember many a lively discussion around the nature-nurture debate and, as I was growing up, it was moving to see the impact she could make on people's lives. It was a vicarious lesson in how to treat one's fellow humans; namely, with understanding, tolerance and compassion. I went on to become a barrister but, when I decided to change from the legal profession in 2012, I seriously considered a career as a forensic psychologist. While I was pregnant with my son, I completed a fast-track Postgraduate Diploma in Psychology and have fond memories of hopping (or waddling) onto the bus from London to Oxford and reading enormous textbooks about neuropsychology on the journey. However, at the same time, I wrote *Holy Island* (my debut novel, and the first in my series of DCI Ryan mysteries) and the rest is history, as they say.

However, I have always maintained an interest in psychology and its application to criminal behaviour. I began to imagine a character who was—first and last—a healer, with a unique capacity to understand criminal behaviour. To that end, I must thank all the eminent psychologists who have provided inspiration through their work in the area, including Paul Britton, David Canter and David Wilson, all of whose books I have greatly enjoyed.

There are numerous other people who have supported me in the making of this book, but none more so than my wonderful husband, James. *Impostor* was a hard book to write; not only because of its content, but because it represents the first book in a new series and a step away from my usual characters. James has been a rock throughout and rightly deserves to be the 'J' in 'LJ Ross' as a permanent thank you for all his help, love, guidance and encouragement.

Thank you to all my family, friends, book bloggers and readers who have followed me over the past four years— I hope you enjoy the story!

If you enjoyed *Impostor*, why not try the bestselling DCI Ryan Mysteries by LJ Ross?

HOLY ISLAND

A DCI RYAN MYSTERY (Book #1)

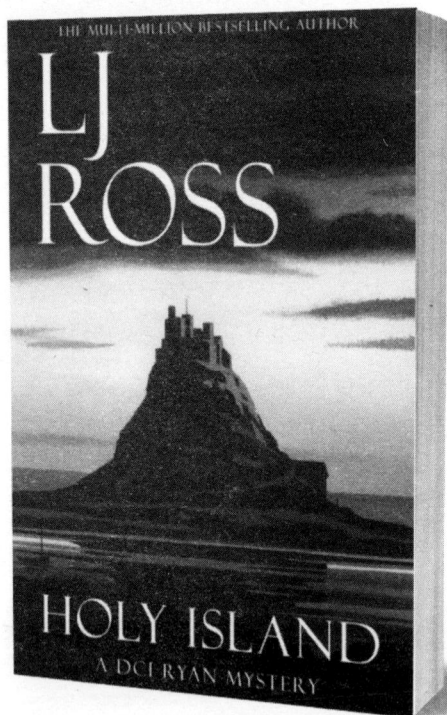

Detective Chief Inspector Ryan retreats to Holy Island seeking sanctuary when he is forced to take sabbatical leave from his duties as a homicide detective. A few days before Christmas, his peace is shattered, and he is thrust back into the murky world of murder when a young woman is found dead amongst the ancient ruins of the nearby Priory.

When former local girl Dr Anna Taylor arrives back on the island as a police consultant, old memories swim to the surface making her confront her difficult past. She and Ryan struggle to work together to hunt a killer who hides in plain sight, while pagan ritual and small-town politics muddy the waters of their investigation.

Murder and mystery are peppered with a sprinkling of romance and humour in this fast-paced crime whodunnit set on the spectacular Northumbrian island of Lindisfarne, cut off from the English mainland by a tidal causeway.

LOVE READING?

JOIN THE CLUB...

Join the LJ Ross Book Club to connect with a thriving community of fellow book lovers! To receive a free monthly newsletter with exclusive author interviews and giveaways, sign up at www.ljrossauthor.com or follow the LJ Ross Book Club on social media:

#LJBookClubTweet

@LJRossAuthor

@ljrossauthor